THE DREAM OF LOVE

Book of Love, Novella

Meara Platt

ARE YOU SIGNED UP FOR DRAGONBLADE'S BLOG?

You'll get the latest news and information on exclusive giveaways, exclusive excerpts, coming releases, sales, free books, cover reveals and more.

Check out our complete list of authors, too!

No spam, no junk. That's a promise!

Sign Up Here

www.dragonbladepublishing.com

Dearest Reader;

Thank you for your support of a small press. At Dragonblade Publishing, we strive to bring you the highest quality Historical Romance from some of the best authors in the business. Without your support, there is no 'us', so we sincerely hope you adore these stories and find some new favorite authors along the way.

Happy Reading!

CEO, Dragonblade Publishing

Additional Dragonblade books by Author Meara Platt

The Moonstone Landing Series
Moonstone Landing

The Book of Love Series
The Look of Love
The Touch of Love
The Taste of Love
The Song of Love
The Scent of Love
The Kiss of Love
The Chance of Love
The Gift of Love
The Heart of Love
The Hope of Love (novella)
The Promise of Love
The Wonder of Love
The Journey of Love
The Dream of Love (novella)
The Treasure of Love
The Dance of Love
The Miracle of Love
The Remembrance of Love (novella)

Dark Gardens Series
Garden of Shadows
Garden of Light
Garden of Dragons
Garden of Destiny
Garden of Angels

The Farthingale Series

If You Wished For Me (A Novella)

The Lyon's Den Connected World
Kiss of the Lyon
The Lyon's Surprise
Lyon in the Rough

Pirates of Britannia Series
Pearls of Fire

De Wolfe Pack: The Series
Nobody's Angel
Kiss an Angel
Bhrodi's Angel

Also from Meara Platt
Aislin
All I Want for Christmas

CHAPTER ONE

Wellesford, England
June 1818

THE FIRST THING to catch the attention of Vicar Adam Carstairs was the sound of the vicarage back door banging open, and the second was the patter of footsteps running down the hall toward his private entrance to the church altar. "Hold there! You! What do you–"

"Look out!" The culprit slammed into him, bounced off his chest, and had barely recovered her balance before avoiding his grasp and running headlong into the church. Yes, it was a *she*. A young and slender *she* if the feel of her body as she'd bounced off him, and the glimpse of her shapely legs as she'd raced into the apse, were any indication.

He hadn't gotten a good look at her, for she had caught him off guard. But it did not take a great intellect to know the whirlwind in white muslin could only be Lady Remington Hartfield giving her father fits again.

"What the...?" He chased after the auburn-haired interloper, spotting her as she dove into the confessional with a bundle in her arms and hastily closed the door behind her.

"Please don't let them know we're in here," she said with a trace of fear in her voice.

We? Ah, the bundle. A rather noisy bundle. He heard thuds, grunts, and bumps as he tried to open the door, but she held it firmly, clinging to it as though her life depended on it. "Please, Vicar!"

The back door banged open once more.

He sighed and moved away. "Very well. Be quiet and keep that thing, whatever it is, quiet."

This time Lord Hartfield and his gamekeeper rushed in, rifles drawn, both men looking as angry as a winter storm off the North Sea. "Where is she? I know she's in here!"

Adam strode forward and blocked their path as they attempted to enter the church. "To whom are you referring?"

The gravel-voiced Earl of Hartfield scowled at him. "Remi, of course. Blasted girl! We'll see how obstinate she remains after I drag her to the woodshed and give her the thrashing she deserves."

"She sprang another of my traps," his gamekeeper explained, shoving Adam aside to enter the church and begin searching behind the altar. "She ain't back here, m'lord."

Adam followed him. "I could have told you that. Get out. You have no business ransacking the Lord's house. That goes for you as well, Lord Hartfield."

The men ignored him and proceeded to peer down each pew.

"I said, get out. Or must I bodily throw the both of you out?" He had the muscle to do it, too. However, as vicar of Wellesford, he supposed he ought to try persuasion rather than brute physical force. Besides, he did not like the apoplectic tinge to Lord Hartfield's face, a sign of his unbridled anger. "You won't find your daughter hiding under the pews."

Which might have convinced the pair had Remi managed to stay quiet. But no, all eyes turned to the confessional as it began to rumble and shake. "A rat infestation, Vicar?" Lord Hartfield muttered, starting toward it.

Adam blocked his path again. "Yes, very large rats," he said, raising his voice to be heard above the noise Remi and her bundle were now making.

The blasted girl.

What was she doing?

It sounded as though Armageddon was going on in there.

She chose the inopportune moment to tumble out of the confessional with an unladylike dive and a feminine "oof" as she tripped over the hem of her gown and landed in a sprawling heap on the stone floor.

The fox she had been protecting took off at a run, slipping through the front entrance, which must have been left ajar by the last parishioners to leave after his morning sermon.

To Adam's surprise, Lord Hartfield and his gamekeeper took off after the fox, sparing not a moment of concern for Hartfield's own daughter, who lay flat on her back, staring up at the ceiling beams.

Adam hurried over to kneel beside her. A few stray curls had fallen over her brow and a streak of sunlight fell across her nose, highlighting the light spray of freckles across its bridge. "Och, Lady Remington," he said softly, revealing a little of the Scottish brogue he preferred to use sparingly since his parishioners seemed to have trouble following his sermons otherwise. Wellesford was a charming town nestled in the Cotswolds, quite removed from his Highland home of Inverness. "This is getting to be a habit with you. Are you hurt?"

"No…not too badly." She rolled to a sitting position. "I may have a rather large bruise forming on my backside. Kindly do not ask to see it."

He grinned. "I won't."

She stared back at him with bright, honey-brown eyes. Doe eyes is how he thought of them, for they were big and round, and framed by the longest black lashes. "Did Kit escape?"

"You named the fox?"

She cast him an impertinent smile. "Not very creative, I will admit. Kit is what they call all baby foxes. But it suits her." She held out both hands to him. "Will you help me up?"

He gathered her in his arms and carefully assisted her to her feet, noticing her wince the moment she put pressure on her right foot. He motioned to the nearest pew. "Sit down. Let me see your ankle. Did you twist it when you fell?"

"Maybe. Why should you care?" She sank onto the wooden bench, which offered no padding for her sore backside. Of course, the girl was too stubborn to admit she was in any discomfort.

He shook his head in exasperation. "Lass, ye cannot keep doing this."

She pursed her lips. They were rather pleasantly shaped lips, pink and full and slightly turned down at the corners in what some might consider an alluring pout. "My father is killing the foxes for sport. I saved Kit from one of his horrible traps."

"Hartfield is his estate. He's entitled to do whatever he wants on it. You shouldn't be walking in his woods. What if you were caught in one of those nasty things?"

She tipped her chin into the air. "It would serve him right, his own daughter lamed because of his traps."

Adam arched an eyebrow. "Seems to me you are the one who will suffer the consequences. What you are doing is dangerous, Lady Remington. You're fortunate you haven't been accidentally shot. You must stop before you are seriously hurt."

As though to prove his point, two shots suddenly rang out.

Her doe eyes rounded in alarm. "He's done it!"

"Wait here. I'll go check."

"I'll go with you." She hopped to her feet and attempted to hobble out, but made it no farther than two pews before she groaned and sank back down in pain. "Please save her, Vicar. Don't let him hurt Kit."

Those shots had been fired by two excellent marksmen at close range. What was the likely outcome? Adam had more sense than to share his thoughts with her. Lady Remington was a hoyden, but she had the face of an angel and a very tender, caring heart. He wasn't sure where she got it from, for her father was a pompous arse and her mother, if the rumors were true, was little better. He'd never met the mother, for Lady Hartfield lived in London while Lord Hartfield enjoyed rusticating in the English countryside.

Apparently, they detested each other.

Remi was the unwanted product of that unholy union.

He knelt beside her once more and tucked a stray curl behind her ear. "I'll try to stop him." *If I'm not too late.* "But promise me you will stay put and not get into further mischief."

"I will. Thank you, Vicar."

The softness in her voice and the trust in her eyes affected him more than he wished to admit. She had such faith in him, and he felt a pang of remorse. "Och, lass, dinna thank me yet. I've done nothing to deserve it."

She stared at him and slowly smiled. "You are doing it again."

He frowned. "Doing what?"

"Slipping into your natural Scottish accent. It's thicker and more rugged than the cultured one you put on. I rather like it. Why do you feel the need to hide your Highland heritage from others?"

"I don't." But he knew she was right. The more important question in his mind was why did he not feel the need to hide it from her? He rose and turned away, unworthy of the openhearted smile with which she'd graced him. "Wait right here. Stay out of trouble." He left the vicarage and turned left down the lane, in the opposite direction from town. If Remi's fox had managed to elude her two pursuers, it meant she had run back into the woods, not toward Wellesford.

The quaint town had become a thriving market destination, always bustling with activity. Survival instinct would have led the fox in the opposite direction.

He walked past Sherbourne Manor, home to the Earl of Welles and his bride, the former Miss Poppy Farthingale. Farther down the lane was Gosling Hall, now home to the Duke of Hartford and his wife, formerly Lady Olivia Gosling, whose father had owned the sprawling country manor and passed it down to her upon his death. Beyond the two estates were Lord Hartfield's manor, park, and woodlands.

He spotted the two men, no more than specks in the distance, and hurried toward them. "Did you catch the fox?"

It did not appear so, for neither man looked pleased and neither carried a fox pelt over his shoulder.

"Blasted creature got away," Lord Hartfield muttered.

"I'll get her next time, don't ye worry, m'lord," his gamekeeper, a large, hard-drinking man by the name of Silas Wilton, assured.

That did little to mollify Remi's father, who now turned angrily to face Adam. "You tell my daughter she needn't come home. If she loves that fox so much, she can sleep in the woods with it tonight." He poked Adam lightly in the chest as he spoke. "Tell her not to come home until she's ready to apologize to me."

Adam knew that would never happen, for Remi was as stubborn as her father.

"She's injured. Twisted her ankle." Adam cast her father a warning glower when he raised his hand to poke him in the chest again.

The man lowered his hand. "I don't care. She's your responsibility now. I'm done with her until I have her apology. And you can tell her if I don't have it by first thing tomorrow morning, I'll...no, I'm not telling you my plans. You'll only help her thwart them. But mark my words, she won't like them."

Nor did Adam like the sound of that threat. "Lord Hartfield, she's your daughter. Won't you reconsider?"

"Hah! I will not." His face was turning that angry shade of purple again. "And I'll tell you another thing, she won't be my problem much longer."

Those spiteful words added to Adam's concern over Remi's welfare. "What do you mean?"

Remi's father cast him a malicious smile. "Remi will soon find out, won't she?"

CHAPTER TWO

LADY REMINGTON HARTFIELD sat in the church pew exactly where the vicar, Adam Carstairs, had left her seemingly hours ago, but it could not have been more than a few minutes earlier that he went chasing after her father, his gamekeeper, and the fox she had been trying to protect. Her hands were tensely folded on her lap as she struggled to maintain her composure. This explained why she did not notice him returning until his shadow suddenly loomed over her.

Remi looked up and sadness burst within her. "They shot Kit, didn't they?"

She had tried her best to save the little thing from the huntsman's trap but had failed. Another win for her father. All she had to show for her efforts was a bruised backside and a sprained ankle that throbbed painfully. "Did she suffer? Or was it a quick kill?"

Vicar Carstairs sank onto the pew beside her. "Kit's safe for now. She got away. Unharmed."

Relief washed over Remi. "But that is a good thing, is it not? Why are you looking so glum?"

He shifted uncomfortably. She hadn't realized quite how big he was. Massive shoulders. Broad chest. A body built for battle. It was odd to see him in his vicar's black garb, but the dark colors suited him. "He doesn't want you coming home until you are ready to apologize for your behavior."

She gasped. "Me? Apologize to him? Never!"

"I thought you'd say as much." He grunted but did not appear put off by her response. "Now, we have to figure out what to do with you until he relents and allows you to return."

She wanted to suggest residing here and helping out with chores, for she was not afraid of working to earn her keep. But she knew it was impossible for several reasons. They were both unmarried. She was not worried about her ruination so much as his. The man had a reputation to uphold. The slightest tarnish and he'd be relieved of his living.

"Would you consider returning to your mother in London?" he suggested.

"No. She sent me up here because she'd had enough of me. I irritate her."

"Why?"

"Why do I irritate her?" She cast him a mirthless smile. "Because I dislike her elegant London society. I cringe at being paraded in front of gentlemen who care nothing for me. I feel like cattle to be purchased at market whenever they inspect me. I'm not in her good favor just now because I am an embarrassment to her. I was sent down from finishing school."

He arched an eyebrow. "Sent down?"

She nodded. "Yes, because I would not curtsy properly or sew a neat stitch to show off my embroidery. My stitchwork is wretchedly poor. But I did learn to laugh with condescension. And cast haughty looks."

He laughed when she gave an example of both.

"I've just turned twenty and am too old to still be in that school. But my mother was not pleased to find me at her door. It was inconvenient for her to have me around, so she sent me up here. I think I irritate her most of all because I resemble my father and she cannot stand to look at me."

"Lady Remi," he said with an ache to his voice, reaching out to take her hand in his. Hers was cold, but his was warm and comforting. "I'm truly sorry."

He was too handsome to resist. Ridiculously handsome, if there was such a thing. Thick, dark hair. A beautifully rugged face to complement his warrior's body. Soulful eyes, the deep blue of a Highland lake, calm on the surface but hiding dangerous undercurrents.

She wasn't the only one whose heart fluttered whenever he drew near. Every woman in Wellesford felt the same about Adam Carstairs. Had a single one of them ever missed his Sunday sermons? It wasn't as though they had all turned pious overnight. Quite the opposite, he brought out the sinful urges in even the saintliest of women.

Not that she was saintly. But she was innocent. Her sins dealt mainly with protecting helpless creatures from her father. She had no experience with men. She had never even kissed a man and had no idea why young ladies were always warned kisses were dangerous. Not that it mattered. She was an oddity, a misfit, and would end her days a spinster. Both her parents thought so, and they never agreed on anything.

He sighed and released her hand. "Let me have a look at your ankle." Without awaiting her reply, he reached down and carefully raised her leg to set it across his lap. "Och, it is badly swollen. Why dinna ye tell me sooner?"

She had upset him. His brogue was prominent again. She particularly loved the way he rolled his r's. *Lady R-r-r-emi*, he would call her, the sound of her name quite delicious as it rolled off his tongue.

She smothered a sigh when he removed her boot and began to run his fingers gently along her foot and up her leg. How many women would die happy in such a position? If she weren't in so much discomfort, she might enjoy the moment. "I unlaced the boot earlier. I didn't think it was that bad," she said and yelped when he touched her ankle. "Ow! What are you doing?"

"Checking for broken bones." Those deep blue eyes of his reflected his exasperation. "You canno' stay here, Lady Remi."

"I know. Are you trying to convince me or yourself? And

please, just call me Remi." It seemed appropriate now that her foot was resting on his muscled thigh. "What may I call you?"

"Vicar Carstairs."

"Ah, ever proper. But since you happen to have your fingers indelicately wrapped around my leg just now, I think I shall call you Adam. Only in private, however. I hope you know I have more sense than to refer to you by your given name in company."

He stared at her swollen ankle. "Let me get you settled in my parlor. Would you care for some tea? You must be hungry. I can offer you a lamb stew or if you prefer something lighter, I have freshly baked bread and lemon cake. I also have an assortment of jams, mustards, root vegetables, and cheeses."

She laughed. "You are a veritable marketplace."

"The ladies of Wellesford believe I need looking after." He shrugged. "I am quite capable of taking care of myself. But I have given up trying to convince them." He picked up the boot he had taken off her injured foot and cast her the sort of look one gave when about to do something unpleasant. "Remi, put your arms around my neck."

The request startled her, but she quickly realized he only meant to carry her into the parlor. It was either that or allow her to hop on her one good foot all the way there. She might have done it, but stairs were involved, and she doubted she could hop up those without falling on her face.

He lifted her as though she weighed no more than a feather, enveloping her in his strong, solid arms. The smart remark she was about to make simply flew out of her head, all her senses now overwhelmed by him.

Her thoughts remained scrambled as he carried her out of the church and into his private quarters. Since her head rested on his shoulder, her lips and nose precariously close to his neck and the firm cut of his jaw, she could not help but inhale the scent of lather from his morning shave and a hint of musk from the cologne he must have put on after his bath.

A pleasant heat emanated from his body, but she dared not burrow into his warmth or allow her hands to roam freely along his muscles. She cleared her throat. "I believe Lord and Lady Welles are in residence at Sherbourne Manor. They are very kind and would take me in if we asked them. Even if they are not at home, his aunt, Lavinia, will be there. We get along very well together."

He nodded. "Let's eat first, and I'll take you over immediately afterward."

He settled her on the sofa, propped a cushion behind her back and another under the injured foot, which he'd now positioned so that it was elevated on the sofa seat. "You have a lot of books," she remarked, rather liking the cozy comfort of the room. There was a desk in the corner, where she imagined he did most of his writing.

"I like to read." He ran fingers through his hair as he stared down at her. "There isn't much else for me to do once I've completed my round of visits to the parishioners. I cannot spend my nights drinking at the local tavern."

"It wouldn't look right. But you don't strike me as the sort who particularly cares what others think of him." She pursed her lips and frowned. "Nor do you strike me as particularly religious or pious. Yet, there is no mistaking you are a good man."

He turned to leave, muttering an excuse about fetching food, but she took hold of his hand. "Adam, what led you to become a vicar?"

"None of your business, Remi."

She took no offense at his curt reply. "Ah, I see you did not like the question. Well, you will like these next ones even less. Have you ever been in love?"

"Also none of your business."

"Is that a yes or a no?"

"Still none of your business."

She took a deep breath and pressed him on the next. "Have you ever considered marrying?"

She expected another mind-your-own-business response as he eased out of her grasp, but he merely stared at her for the longest time. "Never mind about me, lass. Have you ever considered it?"

CHAPTER THREE

"Have I ever considered marrying?" Remi was surprised Adam had turned the question on her. He was now staring at her with his exquisite, assessing blue eyes, awaiting her answer. "I never gave it thought. No one has ever asked me. Why? Are you thinking of–"

"Blessed saints. No, you little snoop. I wasn't proposing to you."

"Because you already have a sweetheart?"

"Never been married or in love," he finally admitted, no doubt to shut her up, as they gobbled down the last of the lemon cake and finished sipping their tea.

Remi understood the sort of man Adam Carstairs was, for one lonely being immediately sensed another's loneliness. However, they were alone for different reasons. She was alone because her parents simply did not like her, and he was alone because he had erected a massive stone fortress around his heart to keep everyone out.

This is why he had never married.

Wellesford's vicar now occupied her mind. She wanted to spend more time with him to learn about his past, but he was obviously eager to be rid of her. As soon as they finished their light repast, he left to saddle his horse. From the window, she could see him lead his magnificent beast, Alcazar, out of the stable and walk him to the back door.

Within moments, she heard Adam's purposeful footsteps coming toward her as he returned to collect her. He would now take her to Sherbourne Manor in the hope of finding her a place to stay for the night. "You ought to let others in, Adam. They won't all hurt or disappoint you."

"What?" He glanced at her, but quickly averted his gaze when lifting her into his arms. He strode back outside, managing to ignore her even though their faces were inches apart. She tried not to stare at him, but he was too handsome to resist, and when would she have such an opportunity again?

He settled her on Alcazar. The steady, gray beast was possibly a remnant of his past. The Scottish cavalry regiment serving the Crown was known as the Scots Greys because of the horses they rode. It was not a leap to believe Adam had been a young soldier during the Napoleonic War.

"People are naturally drawn to you," she said, "but you don't allow anyone close to your heart. Why is that?" He had placed her on the saddle because she was in no condition to walk to Sherbourne Manor on her own two legs. He now held the reins and led the horse at a slow gait in order not to jostle her bruised rump or sprained ankle too badly.

"Stop asking questions. I am not one of your pet creatures to save."

"Who says I am interested in saving you?" She smiled at him when he glanced at her again, his expression startled. "Wanting to understand you is not at all the same thing as wanting to save you."

The noonday sun shone down on them, but a delicate breeze kept the temperature quite pleasant. A short while later, they reached the back gate to Sherbourne Manor. "Adam, we're almost there and you haven't answered any of my questions."

"Nor will I. Stop trying to understand me," he said with a surprisingly angry grumble, shoving the gate open more forcefully than necessary.

She had no response for him, feeling as though she had just

been kicked in the teeth. But he was right. She had overstepped by asking him questions throughout their meal and while making their way to the home of the Earl of Welles.

She was not trying to pry.

She was trying to make a friend and obviously going about it all wrong.

He sighed and turned toward her again. "Sorry, Remi. I was rude to you, and I apologize for that."

"I apologize for irritating you."

He frowned. "You don't irritate me. I am worried about you, lass. That's all."

"I can take care of myself. I have been doing it for most of my life. Rather badly, I suppose. But I have managed on my own thus far."

His hand now rested on the neck of his horse as his tension eased, and he leaned toward her. "That's just it, you haven't. A girl like you ought to have friends. You ought to be going to parties and having young men fall at your feet while spouting odes to your beauty."

"Oh, dear heaven. No." She shook her head and laughed. "I hope to have friends beyond the creatures I spring from my father's traps. I was hoping you would be one of them. As for elegant parties and gentlemen callers, I detest the marriage mart. It is nothing more than a meat market. It holds no allure for me."

"You ought to give it a chance. There are some very good men out there who will appreciate you and wish to marry you."

"Ah, if only this were true." Her laughter faded. "Can you not see how much of a misfit I am? I care nothing for wealth or rank. My parents married for those reasons and look where it has got them. No, what I lack and what I have missed throughout my life is a very important thing called love. This is what I want for myself. Enduring and endearing love. *Love*, Adam. I will not find it in an elegant London meat market."

He regarded her thoughtfully.

When he said nothing, she continued. "I've seen it here in

Wellesford, parents and children who are genuinely fond of each other. I will never forget the radiant happiness in their eyes and in their smiles."

He continued to look at her, his gaze unsettling as he seemed to penetrate her soul. This time she turned away, for her heart was suddenly leaping and bounding as wildly as the fox she had been trying to quiet while hiding in the confessional. It horrified her to think she was developing feelings beyond friendship for the vicar.

She tipped her chin up into the air. "I have resolved to marry for love and settle for nothing less. If I am to have children, I do not want them treated the way I have been treated. Well, you've seen how my parents shuttle me back and forth between them or cart me off to one boarding school or another to keep me out of their sight."

He nodded. "Remi, I want you to promise me something."

She fixed her gaze on him again. "Not to irritate you?"

He chuckled. "No. I've told you already, you do not irritate me. I want you to promise that you will come to me if ever you need to turn to someone for help. I will protect you. Will you remember that?"

"Why are you saying this to me? Has my father threatened something that has you worried? He always threatens, you know. This is his nature. He bullies and blusters. But he is too worried about maintaining his respectable appearance to ever do me any real harm."

"I hope so. He has been drinking more lately."

"I know," she responded quietly. "It is all his unhappiness finally catching up to him."

"Yes, quite likely." He turned away and began leading his horse to the Sherbourne manor house.

She studied him now that he was no longer looking at her. Alcazar snorted and playfully bumped him with his nose as he walked along. "Behave, ye big lump," Adam muttered and took an apple out of his pocket to give it to his steed.

He was a big man, she decided, studying the broad expanse of his shoulders. The muscles he'd built up during his military service had not shriveled in the least and were still prominent.

This was not good.

She had to stop thinking of him in a desirable way.

But she could not find a single fault with him.

Her sigh must have carried on the wind straight to his ears, for he stopped and turned to regard her with concern. "What's the matter now?"

"I was just admiring how well you and your horse get along."

"We have been through a lot together."

"It is obvious in the way you care for each other. Do you know how old I was the first time I realized parents were meant to love their children?" Since he said nothing, merely gazed at her with crystal-blue eyes that seemed eternal in their wisdom, she continued. "I was five years old, and the revelation came to me right here at Sherbourne Manor. Nathaniel's father was still alive and earl then. Olivia's parents and also Poppy's were here that day. I had been invited to a birthday party for Nathaniel's sister, Penelope. We were all close in age, although I was the youngest and quite shy."

"You? Shy?" He arched an eyebrow and grinned in a teasingly affectionate manner that made her heart leap again.

Truly, this feeling had to stop.

"They were sweet, generous girls and treated me as though I was their little sister. Even they noticed my parents were missing from the party. So, they took me by the hand and made certain to include me in all their games. As the afternoon wore on, Poppy and Olivia's parents came over to us and said it was time to take them home. I had never seen parents hug their children before or kiss them. I was startled. As afternoon turned to evening and my father still had not come to pick me up, I began to cry. I thought they would close up the house and leave me outdoors in the dark to fend for myself."

"Och, Remi. Go on, tell me what happened next."

She emitted a ragged breath. "Of course, they did no such thing. I had supper with them and was given one of Penelope's nightgowns to wear to bed since my father had obviously forgotten all about me. Penelope had a big bed, so we shared it. Then an amazing thing occurred. Her father came in, hugged us both, and gave each of us a kiss on the cheek. Then her aunt Lavinia came in and did the same thing. I never forgot that day or those moments."

Adam was not looking at her, but she knew he was listening, so she continued. "I have returned to Sherbourne Manor several times since then and spent afternoons with Penelope and her friends. I hug them whenever I see them, and they hug me back. I don't think they realize how much it means to me."

"I suspect they do. You are not good at hiding your feelings."

Remi sighed. "Truly? I thought I had done a decent job of pretending I do not care."

He turned and cast her a wry smile. "No, lass. You've done a terrible job of it."

"Oh. I see. Well, this is why I must have a husband who will hug me and kiss my cheek each night, and who will do the same with our children. I do not want him ever to forget them, even if he decides to forget me. I don't ever want him to stop loving our children."

They were now at the house, and Adam halted Alcazar at its welcoming front door. Soames, the Sherbourne butler, came out to greet them. At the same time, a young groom came running from the stables to take Adam's horse, but Adam waved him away. "It's all right. I won't be staying long."

He then turned to the butler. "Soames, let the earl and countess know I am here and have brought Lady Remington with me. She is injured."

"At once, Vicar." He hurried back into the house.

Adam placed his hands around Remi's waist to help her down. "Don't try to walk. I'll carry you in."

Since he did not remove his hands once he had set her down,

she did not remove hers from his arms. She had grabbed on to them, only meaning to steady herself. But why hurry to slip her hands off his solid muscles? "No, let me hobble in on my own. If anyone sees me carried in your arms, it will cause an uproar. I may wish to bedevil my father, but I have no wish to embarrass you."

He smiled. "Good to know. Remi, before everyone rushes out, there's just one thing."

She tipped her head in curiosity. "Of course. Anything."

Wordlessly, he wrapped her in his massive arms and hugged her.

She dared not breathe, not even move or blink.

She thought she might shatter when he kissed her on the cheek. "You'll be safe here. But if your father causes you any trouble, summon me. Do you remember what I told you earlier?"

She nodded. "You'll protect me."

He drew away as Poppy and Nathaniel came running out and began to fuss over her. They helped her into their home, and while Poppy continued to fuss over her, Nathaniel led Adam into his private study and shut the door.

Remi was still reeling from his kiss. It was only a gentle kiss on the cheek, but her heart was still in palpitations over it. Did he like her more than he had let on?

Until this moment, she did not think he liked her much at all.

He had brought up her father again and offered to protect her.

Why was he so certain she would need protecting?

An ache tore through her heart.

What was her father planning?

CHAPTER FOUR

"Three days have passed since you brought Remi here," Nathaniel Sherbourne, Earl of Welles, said to Adam as he led him into his study and offered him a seat. "I've sent several messages to Lord Hartfield, letting him know his daughter is here and safe with us. The bounder has yet to respond."

Adam raked a hand through his hair in consternation. Although, why should he be surprised? Hartfield had always treated his daughter wretchedly. "Remi's been subjected to this all her life. It is a wonder she turned out as sweet as she has when both parents behave like infantile terrors."

Nathaniel offered him a glass of sherry to warm his insides from the chill of this unusually wet and blustery June day. It was late afternoon, but the gathering storm clouds had darkened the sky, turning it an ominous grayish black. "Would you care to stay for supper?"

The storm was about to unleash its fury, and Adam wanted to return to the vicarage before the deluge descended upon them. "I'll pass. But I did hope to see Remi. How is she faring? Do you mind her staying with you a little while longer?"

Nathaniel settled in a chair behind his desk and leaned back casually. "She can stay with us for as long as she pleases. We have plenty of room. Poppy and Lavinia enjoy her company. She makes no demands and is no trouble at all."

Adam breathed a sigh of relief. "I don't suppose she intends to apologize to her father anytime soon?"

Nathaniel groaned and shook his head. "No, she will never give him the satisfaction. She's a sweet girl, as you say. But she also has an obstinate streak, no doubt inherited from her father."

Adam frowned.

"What's wrong?"

"Lord Hartfield is up to something. He has been too quiet, don't you think? I had better pay a call on him tomorrow to make certain he isn't planning anything foolish."

"Do you think he means to punish his own daughter beyond merely ignoring her? Has he said anything to make you think so?"

"Not in so many words. Just a vague threat. I dismissed it as the raging of an angry father. His continued silence worries me, however. It means he is sitting and stewing. I would feel more comfortable having him throw another of his apoplectic tantrums to get the anger out of his system." He shook his head. "But this silence…he is like a volcano building up pressure inside of him. I fear what the eruption, when it occurs, will bring."

"Poppy and I will be on our guard. We won't let him be alone with Remi if he attempts to see her." Nathaniel rose. "The ladies must be having tea in the summer parlor at this hour. Shall we join them?"

Adam nodded and glanced out the window again. "Yes, but only a brief visit for me."

He was eager to see Remi for more reasons than simply to ask how she was settling in. When last he'd been with her, she had been going on about the importance of hugs and kisses. Tame kisses on the cheek and innocent, grandfatherly hugs. He had thought to be kind and give her those in parting, telling himself it was the sort of pious gesture a vicar ought to do for a member of his flock whose heart was aching.

What he had not expected was the effect a simple kiss on her cheek would have on him. And when he took her in his arms to hug her, the feel of her body pressed to his was not something he was prepared for. He had never experienced a surge of desire so strong.

Why for Remi?

Yes, she was beautiful…achingly beautiful.

Blast, he had better contain his thoughts or the heavens might open up and angry archangels start hurling lightning bolts down on him.

Keep your hands off the delectable girl.

Well, perhaps angry archangels and lightning bolts were a slight exaggeration. But his heart had been numb for so long, these suddenly strong feelings came as a surprise.

He followed Nathaniel down the hall toward the clatter of teacups and feminine laughter, immediately recognizing Remi's gentle laugh.

His breath caught at the sight of her. She was wearing what had to be a gown borrowed from Poppy, although the pale green silk fit her to perfection, accentuating the soft curves of her body. Her hair was loosely braided and pinned in an intricate twist at the nape of her slender neck.

She was exquisite.

"Adam, how nice to see you." Aunt Lavinia smiled up at him from her perch on the divan beside Remi.

Poppy greeted him warmly as well. "Do come join us. We're just having our tea. What a horrid afternoon. I hope the storm blows over quickly. Will you stay for supper?"

"Your husband asked, but I dare not. Perhaps another time." He turned to Remi. "How are you, Lady Remington?"

She cast him an impertinent grin. "Enjoying myself tremendously and feeling absolutely no guilt for imposing on my friends."

He could see by her expression that she was thinking of their conversation when he'd brought her to Sherbourne Manor, the one about how parents ought to behave toward their children, and husbands and wives ought to behave toward each other. Nathaniel and Poppy were the perfect example of a couple in love.

He thought it might make her wistful not to have this in her life. But quite the opposite seemed true. She glowed with happiness when Nathaniel bent down to kiss his wife's cheek. Whatever love *aura* was floating in the air, Remi was absorbing it and tucking it into her heart.

He sat in a chair opposite the divan and studied her. "How is your ankle?"

"Much better. The swelling has gone down. I no longer have a problem putting pressure on it. I'll be fit enough to dance a jig by tomorrow."

"Good." He cleared his throat, not wanting to broach the topic of her father while in company, but they were not going to be alone anytime soon, and the Sherbournes knew all that was going on anyway. "Is there any message you wish me to convey to your father? I plan on paying him a call tomorrow."

Her smile faded. "You mean any message other than those Lord Welles has sent around and my father has seen fit to ignore? No, I have nothing to say to him." She folded her hands on her lap and stared down at her toes. "It feels different this time, doesn't it?"

Adam did not want to lie to her. "Yes, it does."

She glanced up at Nathaniel. "Lord Welles, I may have to impose on your kindness a little while longer. Not only to remain here but to seek your assistance in claiming whatever is rightfully mine. My father is not going to take me back this time. I feel it in my bones. I already know my mother doesn't want me. Even if she felt any pity toward me, in this she will do as my father commands. He'll threaten to cut off her allowance if she dares to defy him."

She sighed raggedly, and her eyes began to tear. "I should not be feeling so awful. I've been living with this all my life. But even being shuttled back and forth between them feels better than being completely on my own."

Adam reached over and covered her hands with one of his. "You will not be alone. I've told you already, come to me whenever you need help." He glanced at Poppy, Lavinia, and Nathaniel, who all looked quite grim on her behalf.

Nathaniel nodded. "Vicar Carstairs will see your father tomorrow, as he said. We'll decide what to do after they meet. Remi, it is as the vicar says. You are not alone in Wellesford. You, Poppy, Olivia, and Penelope have been friends since childhood. Olivia is now married to the Duke of Hartford. You'll have an earl, a duke, and a vicar to bring pressure on your father to do what's right." He cast her a gentle smile. "And if all else fails, you have Poppy, Olivia, and Penelope to take up arms against your father. He doesn't stand a chance against them."

A roll of thunder sounded in the distance.

Adam slapped his hands on his thighs and rose. "I had better return to the vicarage before the skies open up."

Remi jumped up with him. "I'll see you out. That is…if you don't mind."

"I don't mind. You can tell me what I should convey to your father while you walk me to the door."

"I doubt you'll be willing to repeat what I'd like to tell him. It isn't at all ladylike."

He laughed. "I'll phrase it as politely as I can."

Remi took his arm as they walked out of the summer parlor. He noticed she had no trouble walking, just as she had assured. He was glad the ankle sprain had healed nicely. However, he was surprised Lord Welles had not followed them out. Perhaps Poppy had warned him to stay put and allow them a few minutes alone.

He ignored the ache brought on by having to part from this girl. "I'll see you tomorrow, assuming the storm lets up early enough in the day. I'll come by as soon as I've met with your father."

"Thank you for all you are doing for me." She was staring down at her toes again. "I'm sorry I am such a nuisance."

"You're not a nuisance. This is what I do, Remi. I'm supposed to heal hurt souls." He cupped a finger under her chin and tipped her gaze up to meet his. Then, without thinking, he leaned forward to plant a soft kiss on her cheek.

She threw her arms around him and hugged him fiercely.

He closed his arms around her slender, little body and inhaled the scent of her lavender soap as he buried his face against her neck.

Those damn archangels began tossing lightning bolts at him again. Warning! Warning! Yes, he would burn in the fires of hell if he allowed his lips to touch her skin and his hands to roam where he truly desired over her body.

Eternal damnation seemed worth it at the moment.

It was Remi who drew away first.

Their embrace had lasted no more than a few seconds, but the fire she had ignited in his soul was going to last much longer and simply would not burn itself out. Not even as he rode to the vicarage in a torrential downpour.

Everything around him was drenched and flooded.

But the Remi fire still burned.

What was he going to do about her?

CHAPTER FIVE

THE RAIN HAD stopped by morning, leaving many puddles in its wake. Since the skies were now clear, Remi knew the roads would dry by midday under the heat of the summer sun. This would give Adam plenty of time to visit her father and find out whether he was still too angry to speak to her.

"Remi, you've hardly touched your breakfast," Poppy said, staring at the untouched pile of food on her plate.

"I don't have much of an appetite this morning." She nodded to one of the footmen, who came to take the plate away.

Lavinia lifted her black and tan spaniel, Periwinkle, onto her lap. "Wait! Bring it back," she ordered the man before he could walk off with the coddled eggs and sausage. "No sense letting a good meal go to waste. Right, my sweet baby," she crooned to her pampered dog.

It did not escape Remi's notice that this animal was treated better by Lavinia than Remi had ever been treated by her parents in her entire life.

Poppy must have sensed her distress and cast her a sympathetic smile. "I'm sure Adam will bring your father around. He's smart, eloquent, and can be quite convincing when he puts his mind to it. He also has courage and won't back down if your father shouts and blusters." She glanced out the dining room window. "The rain stopped before dawn. The main roads ought to be clear by now. We shouldn't have too long to wait for news."

To Remi's surprise, Adam rode up to Sherbourne Manor well before midday. Poppy and Lavinia had gone into town to run a quick errand. Poppy's husband, the earl, was off with his estate manager and young ward, Pip, checking his properties for damage after the storm.

Remi had chosen to remain behind with Periwinkle, passing the hours reading in the summer salon while the dog dozed atop her feet, adorably curled in a ball. Eating like a glutton was exhausting work for the little spaniel.

Since Adam had come through the back gate, she was able to see his approach from her position in the salon. Setting aside her book, she eased Periwinkle off her toes and hurried to the entry hall to await him.

She was glad no one else was home, for this allowed her to meet Adam alone and hear his report in private. If the news broke her heart and made her cry, she did not want an audience around her. Knowing her father's nature as well as she did, she did not expect a happy outcome. He did not have a soft heart and would never relent.

The butterflies in her stomach began to flutter and her hands began to tremble as she watched Adam dismount with an easy grace that hinted of years of experience riding. There was something in the way he moved and held himself that made her certain he had spent time in a cavalry regiment, a Scottish one since he called Inverness his home. Why hadn't he returned there after the war? She wanted to ask him and would eventually, but likely not today.

He gave over the reins to the young groom who had run up to attend Alcazar. That he'd allowed the lad to take his horse could only mean this would be an extended visit.

Was this good or bad for her?

"Bad," she muttered, peering out the window and noticing the frown marring Adam's handsome brow. She stood by the door, her anticipation growing as he strode up the front steps.

Soames opened the door to him. "Good morning, Vicar."

"Morning, Soames. Is Lady Remington…" He grinned when she peeked out from behind the butler. "Ah, there you are."

"Have you seen my father?" She put a hand to her stomach to calm its nervous flutter.

"Yes. I suppose you wish to know what he said."

"I do. Shall we walk in the garden? It is a lovely day, and I would enjoy a bit of sun." Also, she did not want their conversation overheard by the Sherbourne staff. They were discreet and trustworthy, but the entire town of Wellesford already knew her father had tossed her out of his home, and she simply could not bear another humiliation.

"Yes, let's take a walk, and I'll tell you about my visit."

They took a full turn around the flower beds before Adam said a word. Remi knew his hesitation did not bode well for her.

She cast him an encouraging smile. "Is the news that bad?"

He pondered the question a long moment before responding. "I'm not sure."

"You're not sure it is bad? Or is it bad, and you're not sure how to tell me?" She studied his features, his dark hair gleaming in the sun and the tense set of his fine, firm jaw. His eyes held her gaze with a power so captivating, they stole her breath away.

"He has decided to marry you off."

"Marry me off?" Remi laughed, at first believing it was a jest. But Adam wasn't smiling. She swallowed hard. "To whom?"

"I don't know." He ran a hand through his hair and sighed. "Your father refused to tell me."

"Can he do this?" She tried not to sound alarmed, but neither her body nor her mind was cooperating. Her heart began to race, her lungs were about to burst, and all her limbs were now shaking. "He cannot just sell me to the highest bidder. I'll refuse. Am I permitted to refuse under law?"

"Were I officiating and the bride proved unwilling, I would not go through with the ceremony. But I doubt I'll be asked to officiate. Your father will find some drunken sloth of a minister to accomplish the task."

"Someone easily bribed who will lie and say I consented?"

Adam arched an eyebrow. "Yes. But before you panic, let me try to find out if he has someone particular in mind. The man might not be so bad."

"Do you really think my father cares if I am happily wed?" She laughed in disbelief.

A muscle twitched in his jaw. "What your father cares about is keeping up appearances, as you've told me yourself. He won't marry you off to just anyone. Likely it will be to a gentleman of rank who is in need of funds to restore his estate."

"Hah! Or just an aristocratic wastrel who will gamble away my dowry."

"No, then he would have you and your wastrel husband back in his house and creditors dunning him everywhere he went. He'll choose someone who may need funds, but who will spend it wisely."

"Or he might cast me off to one of his old-goat friends."

"I hope not. I think not, for it would gain him no advantage. Marriage to a significantly older man would likely leave you a young and wealthy widow over whom he would have no control. I think he has a younger man in mind. This man may even fall in love with you. You are beautiful, Remi. There will be men who will put themselves forward simply because they want you."

Remi shook her head. "Such men do not exist."

"They do." He clasped his hands behind his back as they continued to take another turn around the flower beds. "You just haven't bothered to notice them yet."

"Is it my fault now?" She stopped walking and frowned at him to mark her displeasure.

"No, of course not. All I am suggesting is that not every man is odious."

"So, I should be grateful to my father for choosing the least odious man to marry me?"

"Remi, I am going to throttle ye if ye dinna stop twisting my words," he said, his brogue more pronounced now that he was irritated with her. "Arranged marriages are made all the time. Many of these couples are quite happily wed. Dinna hate the man simply because your father chose him. He might turn out to be someone ye can love."

The fight suddenly went out of her as she realized there was a serious problem. "But Adam…"

"What is it?" He took her hand, running a light circle over it with his thumb to calm her when he noticed her chin wobbling and her eyes beginning to tear.

"I've had so little love in my life."

"Och, I know, lass."

"All I have to go by is what I've seen here at Sherbourne. First when I was a little girl and again now. But these are examples of family love. How will I recognize the other sort of love, that between a woman and a man? Romantic, sweep-me-away-with-kisses love, is what I mean."

He seemed to stop breathing for a moment, staring at her with an intensity borne of confusion. But he soon recovered and cast her a wickedly handsome smile. Well, everything he did was wickedly handsome because this is what he was and every young woman was painfully aware of it. "I was thinking about this very thing while I rode over here. You need someone to teach you about romantic love."

Now it was her turn to stop breathing.

She put a hand over her heart, hoping beyond hope he intended to be the one to teach her. Merciful heaven, was it possible? What would it entail? She was already having sinful thoughts about him.

Were his thoughts about her just as sinful?

He was Wellesford's respected vicar. Would an exchange of kisses corrupt him morally? Would it unleash wanton desires in a physical and morally improper way?

Was it wrong of her to hope for it?

Of course, it was. No wonder her father wanted her out of his house. She was a hoyden and a dissolute. "Who will teach me? You?"

He regarded her oddly. "I was thinking you ought to talk to Poppy. She is happily married to Nathaniel. You can also speak to Olivia, who is obviously in love with her husband, the Duke of Hartford. They're due to return to Gosling Hall tomorrow." He glanced toward the meadow separating Sherbourne Manor from Gosling Hall. "I can assure you, Poppy and Olivia will do all they can to help you understand about this sort of love."

He continued to regard her oddly. "Remi, you look confused. What is the matter?"

She sighed, deciding to tell him the truth since she was not very good at hiding her feelings anyway. "I thought you meant you were going to teach me. Isn't this what you do? Offer guidance to those who are lost?"

His chuckle was deep and resonant. "Blessed saints, not that sort of guidance."

"I'm sorry. I suppose I was not thinking clearly. That sort of love would require some physical involvement, and I know you do not want to touch me in that way. But if marriage is sacred, then isn't there some higher level of awareness and affection that I ought to be taught? An awareness of the senses. You know, sight, touch, taste, scent, and hearing."

He arched an eyebrow. "Who told you this? Poppy? Is she going on about that book of hers?"

Remi shook her head. "What book?"

"Never mind."

"Adam, please tell me. Is this something I can learn from a book? I am an avid reader and a good student when I put my mind to it. Will you tell me? Or must I ask Poppy?"

"No, I'll tell you." He shook his head and groaned. "Have you never seen her toting a book with a faded red leather binding?"

"I hadn't noticed."

"I suppose it doesn't matter. Ask her about it. She is holding on to it for her sister, Violet, when she comes of age. She'll hand it off to Violet when it is time for her to make her London debut. Poppy, Olivia, and Nathaniel's sister, Penelope, claim to have used it to lead each of them to their true love. They are convinced it is magical. But I urge you to ignore that nonsense."

"Are you speaking of the same book they loaned to Miss Billings, the Wellesford bookshop owner? Did she not find true love shortly thereafter with the village doctor?" Her eyes brightened, and she suddenly felt hope about her situation.

He frowned. "The doctor fell in love with her years prior. Indeed, he fell in love with her at first sight. It just took him a while to come around to admitting it."

"But it is no coincidence she happened to be reading this book when he finally found the courage to tell her. The more I think on it, the more it makes sense to ask Poppy for the loan of this book. What have I got to lose? How will I be any worse off? I'll read it, study it. Memorize it. Then I'll know what traits to look for in my perfect husband. She tried to talk to me about the five senses the other day. I ought to have paid closer attention. But it is all in that book, isn't it?"

"Remi, don't place all your hopes on *The Book of Love*."

She inhaled lightly. "A perfect name for it, don't you think? A magical book to help one find love. Adam, this is exactly what I must do, place my hope in it."

"No…that is, I want you to read it. But do not think it is the end all and be all. I do not want to see you crushed."

"I am already crushed. Why should I not pin my dreams on it? Do you have a better suggestion? I need to find the right man and marry him. Elope with him, if necessary. I won't have much time before my father hands me over to the ogre he has chosen for me."

"You're serious, aren't you?" He tucked a finger under her chin to force her to look at him. Oh, she was looking. She could look at him for hours and not blink. If only he knew how perfect he was and how easy it was to stare at him all day. "Do not put all your faith in this…pagan magic."

"But you've seen it work. How can you deny its power?" She slipped out of his grasp and put her hands on her hips. "If it worked for Poppy, Olivia, Penelope, *and* Miss Billings, why do you believe it cannot possibly work for me?"

"Because you would be reading it in desperation and might convince yourself to marry the wrong man simply because he was the first to come along."

"If you are so worried about my inability to distinguish love from desperation, then why won't you help me? You are the one who is supposed to set the example for your parishioners, half of whom are madly in love with you, if you hadn't noticed. And while we are on the topic of marriage, why don't *you* want to get married?"

"Blessed saints! That again?" He folded his arms across his chest and stood with his legs slightly apart, the stance somehow making him appear bigger than he was, and he was already as big and daunting as a warrior knight. "Because I don't. This isn't about me."

"That is not an answer." She had to tip her head back to meet his gaze, for they stood too close now, each of them too stubborn to give an inch. She still had her hands on her hips, and he still had his muscled arms crossed over his chest.

"That is all the answer you are going to get from me. You are the one with the problem, and I am the worst source to offer help. Talk to Poppy."

"I will talk to Poppy after I read her book. If she thinks it is magical, then it must be so. I have no intention of staying ignorant about love."

"We are in agreement on that, so why are you frowning at me?"

"Because I am one of your flock, and you are passing me off on Poppy. Fine, ignore me. Do not feel obliged to lift a finger on my behalf. I'm obviously not all that important to you."

"Blast it, R-r-remi."

Oh, he was rolling his r's again, his heart-melting brogue once again pronounced.

"Indeed, I must be completely insignificant to you. Truly, do not concern yourself. This is my struggle. I must be the one to help myself out of a difficult situation that may impact my happiness for the rest of my life."

He sighed and dropped his hands to his sides. "Lord help us all," he muttered. "Do not look to me to teach you about love. You have no idea what you are asking. I cannot do it, and I will not get involved. Just don't do anything stupid."

"Now you think I am an idiot?"

He groaned. "No, but you are being incredibly pigheaded. Promise me you will come to me before you run off to Gretna Green with some pimple-faced nitwit you hardly know. And promise you will come to me if your father acts on his threat. I won't turn you away. You know that. I will never turn you away."

He gripped her shoulders and stared at her intently. "Are we clear on this? I will not turn you away."

She nodded. "Got it. You won't help me find love, but you will protect me if my father tries to force a man on me."

She felt ashamed for arguing with him. She knew he would continue to press her father, to talk to him and convince him of the right path to take. In the meanwhile, she needed to take her own path, no matter how desperate or foolish he believed her to be for wanting to learn more about this magical book. At worst, she would simply be reading a book. At best, she might miraculously find true love. "Adam, don't be angry."

A deep and aching groan tore from his throat. "I'm not. Just don't go around kissing men because *The Book of Love* encourages it."

She smiled. "I won't kiss just any man. I'll come to you first, as you suggested. You are safe to kiss, aren't you?"

CHAPTER SIX

*S*AFE TO KISS?

Had Remi lost her senses?

Adam ran a hand across the nape of his neck, wondering how their discussion had led the girl to this conclusion. He was the last man she ought to be kissing. He wasn't nearly as resistant to her charms as she believed.

All the more reason to keep his distance. "Well, I had better be on my way. I'll ride over to your father's place again tomorrow. Perhaps he will have calmed down by then."

She nodded. "I am being ungracious. I truly thank you for all you are doing. We both know this will not have a happy outcome unless I crawl back to him on bended knee. It will destroy a piece of my soul to do it, but I may have no other choice. I cannot remain a burden to Poppy and Nathaniel for much longer. Nor will I agree to spend my life going from friend to friend, living off their largesse."

She shook her head and laughed. "I only have three I would consider friends, Poppy, Olivia, and Penelope. I did not see them often enough to really become close, so how can I impose on them when they hardly know me?"

He caressed her cheek, a mistake for certain. But the sun was shining down on the beautiful girl, catching the fiery auburn highlights of her hair. Her eyes were glistening with unshed tears, and he could not bear for her to cry.

Remi had spirit, but her father was doing his best to pound it out of her.

"Count me as a friend, as well," he said, unable to tear his gaze away from her expressive eyes. He'd never seen eyes quite that golden brown, the gold in them making them appear luminescent.

She emitted a shaky laugh. "Well, in that case…friend. Would you care to stay for lunch? Poppy and Lavinia will be back shortly. I expect Nathaniel will return as well. He took his young ward, Pip, along with him on his inspection of the storm damage. I doubt they'll stay out all day."

"Another time." Because he was going to kiss her if he stayed in her company any longer.

She did not hide her disappointment. "Of course. I understand."

They walked back to the house, and she accompanied him to the front door. They were standing on the steps waiting for the Sherbourne groom to bring Alcazar around when she noticed a wagon coming up the drive. "That's Mr. Langley, one of my father's retainers. Do you think he's been sent to bring me home?"

Adam put a hand around her waist and drew her close, an instinctively protective response. The girl wore her heart on her sleeve, wanting so badly for her father to love her. Adam dreaded what would come next, for this man driving the Hartfield wagon looked grim.

Remi was too hopeful to notice. "Good morning, Mr. Langley. Has my father sent you for me?"

The man looked ashamed. "No, Lady Remi. He told me to bring ye these." He motioned to the pile of clothes dumped onto the back of his wagon without care. "And he told me to give ye this letter. I'm truly sorry, m'lady."

Remi's hands were shaking so badly, Adam reached for the letter on her behalf. "Thank you, I'll take it." He then turned to the Sherbourne butler. "Soames, see to bringing Lady Remington's things upstairs."

The man nodded. "At once, Vicar."

Adam kept his arm around Remi as the staff gathered her belongings and marched back into the house with them. He continued to hold her while they remained standing on the front steps watching Mr. Langley drive the wagon out of sight of the manor. Only then did Remi emit a ragged sigh and turn to face him. "Well, at least I'll have my own gowns now and won't have to borrow Poppy's."

Then her composure completely crumbled. She ran off toward the shaded walk beyond the flower garden, where they had just been talking. It was a spot hidden from view of the house. Adam kept a small distance behind her, wanting to give her time to exhaust her frustration. She finally came to a halt amid a copse of gracefully arched trees and covered her face with her hands.

She was sobbing by the time he reached her side.

He took her in his arms and held her tightly, cradling her as she rested her head against his chest. "We'll work it out, Remi."

She tipped her head up to stare at him, although he doubted she could see much beyond her wall of tears. "How? All I wanted to do was make him see the cruelty of his traps. But he thinks as little of me as he does of the animals he snares in those iron claws. And my mother doesn't think of me at all. Am I that wretched a person, Adam? Why do they hate me so much?"

"They hate each other. You've got yourself caught in the crossfire." And now he'd gotten himself caught in something unexpected, as well. Remi's body felt splendid pressed against his, quite right and perfect. It was more than the mere physical pleasure of it. Yes, her body was soft and nicely shaped.

But the yearning she stirred in him was like nothing he'd ever experienced before. It was as though the girl had hurled boulders off a catapult straight at the walls he'd built around his heart. She was crushing them, battering them down. Demolishing them.

Making him *feel* again.

Only, he had never felt like this before, not even in the years before he'd defied his father's wishes and gone off to war. The horrors of war had numbed him and left him empty of sensation in all the years afterward.

Until now.

Mother in heaven.

Remi's hair felt silky to the touch. He wanted to run his fingers through her unruly curls and run his tongue along the curve of her sweet mouth. As he leaned closer to breathe her in, he caught the scent of lavender on her skin and the scent of honey on her lips.

She would have him out of control if he wasn't careful.

He ached to crush his mouth to hers in an endless kiss. But he knew he would never have the strength to pull away from her once their lips met. "Come, Remi. Let's sit by the river and read the letter together. We'll come up with a plan to bedevil your father."

She nodded, making no protest as he took her hand in his. Even the touch of her hand felt perfect and sweet, the way her slender fingers trustingly entwined with his. His hand was big enough to swallow hers up as they walked across the meadow toward the river running behind the neighboring Gosling Hall. They'd be alone back there, away from prying eyes and straining ears. No one to hear or see if either of them said or did something foolish that was better left forgotten.

While the sun had dried much of the area, there remained small puddles and muddy patches, especially as they drew closer to the bank of the river. Perhaps it was not one of his brightest ideas, but privacy was more important than comfort at the moment. The wooden bench beside the swiftly flowing waters was still damp from last night's rain, so he removed his jacket and placed it over the moist planks for Remi to sit on. "But your coat will get wet."

He smiled. "But your dainty backside won't."

She managed a laugh.

"Sit down, Remi. Do you want me to read the letter to myself first?"

"No, let's read it together. You needn't protect me, I'm used to this treatment," she said as he settled beside her. "I thought things might improve as I got older, but I fear it is just getting worse."

The paper crinkled in Adam's hands as he unfolded it. "My dear Lady Remington," he said, reading the letter aloud and wondering at Hartfield's formality in addressing his own daughter, "I had thought your becoming a young lady would improve your temperament. But I see you remain as spoiled and ungrateful as your mother despite all I have done for you. So, I will not mince words. If you do not apologize to me within a week's time, I am disowning you–"

Adam broke off and turned to face her. "Remi, I will speak to him. I will make him see reason."

"Don't waste your breath on my account. He is intractable. Once his mind is made up, he will not change it. Please, there's more. Let's read the rest."

He sighed heavily and nodded. "Do not think to plead to your mother. I have already written to her threatening to cut off her allowance if she takes you in. Begging her will do you no good, for she will always choose her comfort over yours."

Adam stared at the letter, wanting to burn the odious thing and beat her father to a bloody pulp. As vicar, it was probably not the wisest course of action, but he had also been a soldier in the Napoleonic Wars. That need to fight and protect was in his blood and in his soul.

When Remi placed her hand over his, he realized it was because he had been trembling with rage and she was attempting to soothe him. *Blessed saints!* Despite her world falling apart, she still worried about him. He should not have been surprised, for Remi's heart was soft and tender toward all creatures.

She continued to read, for he was too overcome with anger to do it. "Once this week is up, you need never contact me again. I will not accept you back into my home. It will be as though you died."

"Wretched man," Adam muttered.

Remi made no comment as she read on. "From that moment on, you shall be alone in the world. Find your own husband, although I am certain no one will have you without a dowry. Perhaps a dose of the harsh realities of life will humble you. If you do come home within the week and show me the proper respect, I shall provide a husband for you and a suitable dowry. The choice is yours. One week."

Her father had signed it and added his seal.

Adam took the letter out of her hands because she was simply staring at it, and this troubled him. "We'll figure out something, Remi."

She refused to look at him and now stared at the river current as it swept past them with a steady *whoosh, whoosh*. "What are my choices? He will undermine my attempts to find work as a companion or governess. He will cut me off at the knees if I attempt to be independent of him. So, what must I do? Grovel to him and hope he will not foist an ogre on me to wed? It is either that or find myself a husband I can tolerate. But I must find him before the week is out. How is it possible?"

She finally turned to look at him. "I'm sorry, Adam. I wish I was stronger, but the prospect of being penniless and alone terrifies me."

"As it would anyone."

She shook her head. "Not you. I don't think you are afraid of anything."

He frowned. "Why do you say that?"

"Because I think our situations are a lot more alike than you let on. Why did you leave Inverness? Why have you not gone back there after the war? What horrors did you experience during the war that turned you into a vicar? A vicar, I might add, who preached faith to his flock, and all the while he lacked it."

"That isn't so. I got my sign of faith. I no longer doubt."

His admission surprised her. "Oh, Adam. Then I'm glad for

you. But I hold out little hope for myself. I am not afraid of hard work, but he will thwart me in anything I attempt to do. So far he has not bothered my friends, but I fear that will change after next week. How can I stay with Poppy and Nathaniel if my father will unleash his anger on them?"

"Nathaniel isn't afraid of him."

"Even so, what sort of friend am I to bring this unpleasantness into their home? No, I need a miracle in the form of a husband, especially one I can love. I'll read Poppy's book this very day. I'll grasp at anything. Do you think miracles can happen in less than a week?"

CHAPTER SEVEN

REMI HAD GIVEN her marriage prospects plenty of thought and came to a decision by the following day.

She was going to marry Adam Carstairs.

But how was she to make him fall in love with her in six short days?

Remi pondered this very thing as she took afternoon tea with Poppy, Lavinia, and their neighbor Olivia, the Duchess of Hartford, in the Sherbourne parlor. Last night she'd told them about her father's ultimatum and admitted how she felt about the Wellesford vicar.

Poppy had leaped out of her chair, raced upstairs, and returned with the magic book in hand. She gave it to Remi with the most solemn look she'd ever seen on her friend. *The Book of Love,* Poppy had whispered as though it were a priceless treasure, "will lead you to your true love. You must read it immediately."

She had started it last night and read through much of it. "I had no idea men and women approached love so differently."

"You should have seen me and Beast," Olivia said with a light laugh, referring to her husband, the Duke of Hartford, who behaved more like a besotted lamb around his wife even though he was big and daunting, made even more so by the black eyepatch he wore over the eye he'd lost fighting Napoleon. "Getting him to see me as a desirable woman instead of a childhood friend took delicate planning."

"We approached it as a battle plan worthy of Waterloo," Poppy said. "Fortunately for us, men are easily manipulated when under the influence of their lustful urges. And they are always under the influence of those urges. This is how they are made. They cannot help themselves. But it is their ability to love that civilizes them."

Remi was hesitant. "Adam is a vicar. Is he allowed to feel lust? And don't I need him to feel something more for me? I cannot marry him if he does not love me. I cannot trick him into it by powerful magic."

Olivia shook her head. "No, there are no love spells, just...*recipes*, I would call them, for want of a better word. You would not be forcing him to do anything he was not ready or willing to do."

"Are you certain? Because it wouldn't be fair to him."

Poppy nibbled her lip. "What you need is a plan to make him see what is before his very eyes. Right now, he is refusing to look at you clearly. Believe me, this is quite common. What we need to do is find someone to make him jealous. Competition is certain to bring out his possessive instincts. If he cares for you, then you will know it as soon as another man shows you any interest because Adam will turn into a protective ape and chase this man away."

Olivia grinned. "Yes, he will seethe and glower at every man who comes near you. This is the wonderful thing about a man's nature."

"Even Adam's? He seems to keep his feelings under tight control."

"Yes, even him," Olivia assured. "Poppy, Penelope, and I went through this and can state with confidence that men are at heart simple creatures. They will always respond on instinct. If you are meant to be his, you will know it well before the end of the party."

"What party?"

"The one we shall hold for you," Lavinia intoned with cheer. "We must invite all the eligible young men in Wellesford. After all, if you do not make the choice, then your father will make it for you. That is unacceptable. We must not allow this to happen."

Olivia and Poppy nodded enthusiastically.

"Too bad Penelope isn't here. She'll be so disappointed not to be in on the plot," Poppy said.

"It is not a plot, merely a nudge in the right direction," Lavinia insisted. "It is not our fault men are dense and need to be nudged."

"A swift kick in the pants is what he needs," Olivia muttered.

Lavinia ignored the comment and addressed Remi. "You are not taking advantage of him. You…we…are all thinking of his happiness, too."

Remi groaned. "This is going to be humiliating. Every man invited will know the reason for the party, and if no one steps forward, then I'll be a laughingstock and can never show my face in Wellesford again."

"Dozens will come forward," Lavinia said, feeding her precious Periwinkle a sliver of her scone as the pampered pup lounged on her lap. "Do you not realize how pretty you are, Remi? Not merely in looks but in compassion. The vicar is drawn to you. He cannot help himself."

"He doesn't want anything to do with *The Book of Love*. He told me so himself. He'll be angry and keep his distance."

Poppy quietly spoke again. "Trying to move Adam's heart will be like trying to move the twelve-foot-thick walls of an impregnable fortress. Nathaniel was the same way. War scars men, and it is nothing to be taken lightly. They respond to those scars in different ways, as well. Adam has built those thick walls because he does not ever wish to feel again. The pain of loss still haunts him, I'm sure. So, he hides from any serious commitment. If he cares for no one, he can never be hurt again."

"But at the same time, he longs to feel love," Olivia said. "His walls can be surmounted."

Lavinia huffed. "Surmounted? I should say not. Remi must blast cannonballs through them. Destroy them entirely."

Remi cleared her throat and began to fidget because she was feeling decidedly uncomfortable with this plan. And yet...if it worked, all her dreams would come true. The fact was, Adam had been in her dreams from the moment she'd met him. "A party it is. When shall this affair be held?"

Poppy arched an eyebrow. "You have six days left to respond to your father. This party will take some planning. Orchestra, food, invitations sent, furniture moved. We shall hold it in five days."

"Leave everything to us," Olivia said. "In the meanwhile, you must not stay idle. Adam needs to be softened up. You know what I mean, don't you?"

Remi shook her head in dismay. "No."

Olivia reached over and patted her hand. "Nor did I, but with the help of that book, I managed to gain a proposal of marriage from Beast."

"How am I to accomplish this? Adam has rebuffed every woman in Wellesford." She turned to Poppy. "Except I think he would have married you if you hadn't fallen in love with Nathaniel and married him instead."

"No." Poppy was quite adamant. "Never believe those rumors. He was polite to me and perhaps for a moment thought I had the right temperament to be a vicar's wife, but it was never about him losing his heart to me. He was only thinking of a possible match in the event he received pressure to find himself a wife."

Poppy and Olivia were now grinning at her.

"Oh, stop it. You just said he was considering you because of your sweet and quiet nature, Poppy. I am the opposite of quiet. I ruffle everyone's feathers."

"Well, you ruffle something in him," Lavinia remarked dryly. "One has only to look at his eyes when he's around you. That icy blue gaze he is famous for turns to blue fire when he looks at you. Mark my words. I have been around men long enough to know heat and desire when I see it."

Remi laughed. "You have been reading too many of those naughty novels, Lavinia."

"Perhaps, but you must promise me you will continue to read the book Poppy gave you. If you want your miracle to happen, then take your task seriously and pore over every chapter."

"I will. I promise." Holding the faded leather tome in her hands last night had not made her feel differently. Her fingers had not tingled. The butterflies in her stomach had not fluttered. But who was to say how its magic worked?

After tea, she walked to the garden with the book in hand. She intended to read it quietly out here, but Nathaniel and Pip were talking to his gardeners, so she continued past them to the river. The sun had been shining all day, and any lingering puddles or patches of mud were long gone. Also, there was something quite soothing about the river's flow and the gentle afternoon breeze.

She would move the bench to a shady spot under a tree and read.

To her surprise, Adam was already seated on the bench when she arrived, his size leaving little space for her. She studied him as he stared at the crystal waters flowing southward with the current.

He seemed lost in thought, so she hesitated to approach him.

There may have been a little cowardice involved, too. Especially now that she understood more about men and women and what drew them to each other. Love was fragile. There were so many ways it could fall apart. Her parents were an obvious example, although she doubted they had ever been in love.

Mutual hatred from the moment they first set eyes on each other. Yet, this had not stopped them from marrying.

A twig crunched under her foot, drawing Adam's attention. "Remi?"

She nodded. "I did not mean to disturb you. I came here to read, but I'll find myself another spot."

He rose and came toward her, seeming to dominate the entire outdoors as he strode to her side. He arched an eyebrow when he noticed the book she held.

Did he just wince?

He took her hand. "No, stay. I only needed a moment here. You may have the place to yourself."

"I wish you would stay with me. We can read the book together."

You would think she had just suggested they eat worms, he looked that horrified. "I am not reading that book."

"Why? Are you afraid of it?"

"Of a book?"

"Of the truth it will reveal about kissing and touching and falling in love. Everyone needs to feel loved. I am desperate for it, as you well know. And you are desperate to hide from it. Why are you here, Adam?"

He glanced around the scenic spot. "Lovely day. Quiet of the woods. Good for a moment's reflection."

"No, I mean, why are you in Wellesford and not with your family in Inverness?"

"That again. Not a topic for discussion. I'll see you tomorrow, Remi."

"Please don't go. I won't ask you any more questions. I'll set the book aside for now. Just stay with me, please."

He sighed but gave a curt nod.

She smiled back, hoping he would not notice how completely he overwhelmed her senses. Everything about him was perfect.

How was she ever going to make him kiss her?

Perhaps she would build up the courage over the next few days. "The Sherbournes have decided to throw me a party." She followed him when he moved to stand beside the riverbank. "You'll be invited, of course. Promise me you will attend."

He nodded and returned his gaze to the water. "I'll be there."

It was little more than a gently flowing stream, but it represented something to Adam. Perhaps the swift currents of life. How fleeting their existence.

"Poppy and Olivia are convinced I'll find a man who will marry me at the party. I mean, not marry me then and there, but who will want to marry me."

"Then your father will no longer be a threat to you?"

"He'll always be a threat. Men may want to marry me, but few are strong enough to defy him. I don't have the heart to tell Poppy and Olivia their party will likely fail. They have been so kind to me." She took off her shoes and stockings and set them on the bench beside her book.

He frowned. "What are you doing?"

"Am I not allowed to dip my feet in the water?" She carefully waded in. "Oh! It's cold! But it feels so good. Come in with me."

Adam's smile reached into the silvery-blue depths of his eyes. "No, I prefer watching you."

She could have uttered a comment about how this is what he was doing with his life, standing aside, watching it stream by. Never jumping in. Never making a fool of himself…as she was about to do, for something long and wriggling just moved through her legs.

She screamed and tried to dart away from it but slipped and fell into the shallow water. Her head went under for just a few seconds before Adam caught her up in his arms and carried her to shore. "Remi, lass! Och, are ye all right?"

Ah, the protective Scot was back. But it took her a moment to stop sputtering and coughing before she could reply. "I think so."

Her hair was soaked and falling over her face, so she took out the sagging pins, shook it out, and ran her fingers through it to brush the wet mass off her face. Her gown was clinging to her body. There was nothing she could do about it now. "Adam, I think something scratched my leg."

"Let me see." He set her down on the bench and lifted her gown as high as her knees. "Where, Remi?"

"My right calf. Perhaps it was only a trout rubbing against me. It startled me."

"Did you feel a bite?" He cupped her leg in the palm of his hand and turned it slightly to inspect it. "I see scratches but no puncture wound."

"I don't think it bit me, just brushed against me. Oh, my goodness! Do you think it was a snake?"

"No, just a fish. Even if it was a snake, there are no poisonous ones around here." He ran his fingers lightly along her skin. No snake bite would kill her, but his divine touch just might. Her heart was thumping so hard, it threatened to burst within her chest.

Fortunately, Adam was studying her legs and not her heaving bosom—an expression she'd learned from one of Lavinia's naughty books. "You have a nasty scrape, Remi. The scratches are deep and broke through your skin. There's a little blood. Let me wipe it off you."

He withdrew a handkerchief from inside his pocket, pressed it lightly against her leg, and tied the handkerchief around it to form a makeshift bandage.

Then he looked up at her.

It was as though everything stopped in that moment. The wind no longer rustled through the trees. The birds stopped chirping. The water currents stilled. "Um, Adam. Will you help me back to Sherbourne Manor? Perhaps take me in through the servants' entrance. I'm soaked and–"

"Remi, stop talking." His big hand cupped her face, and he slowly eased closer to her.

"I only wish to explain that I'm wet and shouldn't–"

"Stop talking."

"Why?"

"Because I am going to kiss you."

CHAPTER EIGHT

ADAM WAS GOING to kiss her!

Remi wanted to close her eyes, but at the same time wanted to keep them open to see what he was doing and learn from it. She had dreamed of him kissing her in a moonlit garden, but here by the river, in the sunshine, under a light breeze and birds chirping in the trees, could not be more perfect.

Except she was soaking wet, having slipped by the edge of the water and fallen under completely.

No one said she had to look perfect to be kissed.

And this was truer to her nature, for she had never been the biddable, sit-in-the-parlor-and-behave-like-a-proper-lady sort of girl.

Adam cupped her face in his hands and smiled at her.

She was going to savor the moment, for this might be the only kiss she would ever receive from him. Even if he regretted it and never spoke to her again…well, no, she wanted them to speak again. She wanted him to marry her and kiss her endlessly, but she would worry about that later.

She closed her eyes, deciding he was less likely to change his mind if she did not look him directly in the eyes. Besides, she was growing cold in these wet clothes and feeling the breeze against them. She wanted him to kiss her before her lips turned blue.

"Remi," he said in an aching whisper, the one raspy word starting a little fire in her body that chased away her chill. He cupped the back of her head and circled his arm about her waist to draw her up against him.

He was getting his front all wet.

He did not seem to care.

His lips came down on hers, pressing against her mouth with surprising ardor, his kiss confident and deep. This was not a polite kiss, by any means. Nor was it too rough, just filled with smoldering heat and overwhelming tenderness.

She wrapped her arms around his neck and returned his kiss with equal intensity. She could be no other way with him. His lips were warm and his tongue felt delicious as it licked along the seam of her mouth. He did no more than lick lightly, perhaps not wishing to scare her with his passion. He was holding back, not giving his urges free rein.

That he felt *any* urges with her was rewarding enough.

"Remi, stop thinking," he said in an amused whisper against her lips. "Just feel the kiss. Let it flow through you."

She wanted to tell him to do the same, for he was the one hiding from his feelings. Hers were so open and exposed, it was at times humiliating. But she wasn't about to lecture him, not while she was wrapped in his muscled arms, her head resting against his hard, solid chest, and her lips hungrily probing and tangling with his.

She was trying to reach his soul.

He may only have been thinking of her body, but she wanted all of him.

Not that she minded surrendering only her body. She felt drawn into a fiery whirlpool of desire, her senses heightened and her heart eager to take all of him in. She had read those chapters on the five senses and given him top marks in each category.

The look of him was splendid, of course. Masculine and magnificent. The scent of him also stirred her senses. She inhaled the sandalwood and rugged outdoors scent of his skin. The taste of him, of the strawberry jam he must have eaten this morning and washed down with his coffee.

He growled low in his throat, the sound possessive and sensual as he ended the kiss. "Remi, I can *hear* your mind racing."

"No, Adam. You are mistaken," she said in a whisper, hardly able to catch her breath. "You've left me mindless. I am feeling each sensation."

"What do you mean?"

"The senses. I've gotten through the first four, sight, taste, hearing, and scent. I was just getting to the sense of touch, but you ended the kiss before I was finished."

"You are still in my arms. How does my touch feel?"

"Do you really need to ask? I would stay right here forever if I could. I would hold on to you and love you all the days of my life if you ever let me."

She recognized her mistake at once. She had mentioned love.

He stiffened and drew away.

Now out of his arms, she began to shiver.

He glanced at her and noticed she'd wrapped her arms around herself. "Bollocks. You're shaking."

"From cold," she assured. "I am not about to cry because you don't love me. I never dared hope you would be the one to marry me. Well, I did consider it. Dreamed of it. Then quickly squashed it. I have no intention of lying to you or to myself. If the choice were mine to make, I would choose you. I would not be choosing you for your good looks, either. Although we all know how stunningly handsome you are. I would be choosing you for your kindness. For your strength and compassion. For your ability to think for yourself and stand up for what is right."

He removed his jacket and wrapped it around her. "Let me take you back to the manor house. The wind is cooling. You should not stay out here much longer. Lord, you look like a drowned water rat."

He was staring at her, that stony, expressionless look she detested, even more so at this moment. He was hiding his feelings again, retreating behind that massive wall around his heart. As for her, she had never built any walls.

No, she was completely defenseless. *Step right in. Trample my heart. Stomp on it. Stomp on it harder. Leave it in tatters.*

"Remi, I–"

"If you dare tell me our kiss was a mistake, I vow I shall punch you in the face." She curled her hands into fists, not that he would notice. His jacket was far too big for her, and the sleeves fell below her hands.

He laughed, and his gaze turned tender. "No, I would never say that. What I was going to say before you turned Valkyrie on me and threatened to beat me to a bloody pulp was, would you come help me at the vicarage tomorrow?"

She inhaled lightly. "Yes, of course. Why?"

"The church council wishes to plan something for Midsummer's Eve. You're more creative than I'll ever be. Why don't you come along and have a listen? Maybe offer a few suggestions."

She wasn't certain why he'd asked her, but she had only a few days to figure out her life and already knew that Adam had to be in it. If he wanted her at the vicarage, she would show up promptly at the scheduled time, dressed demurely, but not so demurely he would not notice her body and perhaps ache a little over it. "You are asking for my ideas?" She grinned at him. "They might be outrageous."

He arched an eyebrow and grinned. "I am fully aware and am counting on it. You'll offer something fun for all. Every year it is a stodgy, holier-than-thou event everyone must suffer through to prove how pious they are. As you know from the kiss we just shared–"

"Did you like it, by the way?"

His smile melted her heart. "Yes."

"I'm glad. I liked it very much, too."

"I know." He nodded toward the bench where the book and her stockings were still perched. "Midsummer's Eve is a pagan holiday, which is why the council wants everyone praying in church instead of out in the fields, stark naked and howling at the moon."

"That sounds ever more fun."

He caressed her cheek. "It would be with you. But the thought of all my parishioners stripped down to nothing, their pasty arses flapping in the moonlight..." He gave a mock shudder. "It would haunt my dreams."

"And they're already haunted, aren't they?"

His face drained of color in that moment.

"Adam, I'm sorry. I've opened my big mouth again. Don't be angry with me. I've already told you that I want to make a life with you. I've told you that I love you. I'm not taking it back and will never deny it. Never. If we married, which would be a holy miracle, I know. But if we married, I would never withhold anything from you. I would never lie to you. I would always confide in you because I trust you and value your opinions. I know you'll tell me the truth and always protect me. You'd be my friend and my solid rock, just as I would be yours."

He stalked to the bench, picked up the book, her stockings, and her shoes, then marched back to her and dumped them in her hands. Was he going to leave her and tell her to make her own way back?

He answered by lifting her in his arms and carrying her toward the manor house. "I merely invited you to a council meeting," he said with a growl.

"No, you didn't. You invited me into your church. Into your sanctuary, which is a metaphor for your heart."

"Amazing. You discerned all that from a simple invitation?"

"Yes." She rested her head against his shoulder, her ear picking up the steady beat of his heart. "You want me in there." She touched him lightly, placing her palm flat against his heart for a moment before she drew it away. "You'd just like those walls to come down a little slower, allow me to remove a stone here and a stone there. But you're wondering if you can let me in without showing me all of you."

"Can I?"

She nodded. "Yes, I will not push you. When you are ready, I know you will tell me. And if you are never ready, that will be all right, too." She glanced at *The Book of Love*. "I told you I'm an avid reader and a good student when I want to be. This book isn't a magical book of spells, it is a pathway to the magic that happens when you open your heart to love."

He grumbled but was still listening, so she continued. "This is why several chapters are devoted to exploring one's senses. We have to be taught to look and listen, to touch with kindness and speak with truth. I wish I could give this book to my father, but he'd toss it into the fire and burn it. Anyway, it isn't mine to give away. I'll return it to Poppy before the party."

He did not look pleased at the mention of a party.

Good. She wanted him to be possessive and apelike when suitors came forward. She wasn't certain any would, but several men might ask her to dance. Hopefully, it would be enough to rile Adam. She wanted him in that piss-in-the-corners-to-mark-his-territory state of arousal. She wanted him to pound on his chest like a barbarian and declare no one but he would ever touch her.

Well, she was exaggerating quite a bit.

Neither of them spoke as they made their way back until Adam suddenly broke the silence. "I had four older brothers."

She inhaled lightly. "Any younger brothers? Any sisters?"

"No."

"So only the four older brothers. Are they all in Inverness?" She asked the question warily, afraid she would scare him off if she asked more. But she wanted to know about his family, his childhood, anything he would share with her.

"Yes…I suppose one could say that."

"Wait, you said *had* four. Adam, I'm so sorry. Is this the reason you aren't with your family now?"

She could hear the turmoil in his silence.

"What happened to your brothers?"

CHAPTER NINE

REMI TOOK GREAT care in choosing the perfect gown to wear for her afternoon meeting at the vicarage. Adam had invited her yesterday to participate in the midsummer celebration discussions, and she did not wish to be late. In truth, she had considered arriving early to learn more about his Inverness family, especially knowing that he'd lost brothers in the war, but decided to linger afterward to pose her questions. To do so before the meeting would not be productive and might only aggravate him.

After opening his heart just enough to mention he had four brothers, he'd slammed it shut again and told her nothing more. She was patient and could wait him out, assuming her father did not haul her away and force her to marry a toady of his choice. "Good afternoon, everyone. I hope I'm not late."

Adam seemed relieved to see her. "No, you are right on time."

He rose from his seat in the parlor and offered it to her, giving her arm a little squeeze, which she took to mean he was glad to see her.

"I think you know Lady Monkton." He nodded toward an elegantly dressed blonde in her early thirties.

"I do. How are you, Lady Monkton?" Remi was sorry she and Adam would not have a moment alone. Perhaps he would agree to walk her back to Sherbourne Manor, then they could talk as they sauntered along the road. Yes, it was better to get him away from the vicarage, where he could come up with any feeble excuse to be rid of her and not answer more of her questions.

"Quite well. And you, Lady Remington? I understand you've landed in a spot of trouble yet again."

It was a snide comment to make, but Remi tried to overlook her smirk and the way her chin was raised as though peering down her nose at Remi. "No, all is well." She was not about to rise to the woman's bait. "I'm so pleased Vicar Carstairs thought to ask me to your meeting."

She turned to the other two ladies seated in Adam's parlor. "Good afternoon, Mrs. Dowd. Miss Dowd. It is a lovely day, isn't it?"

"Too warm for my liking," said Mrs. Dowd, taking out her fan and waving it across her face so that her body odor wafted through the room. It wasn't a very pleasant odor, which immediately brought *The Book of Love* and its chapter on the sense of smell to Remi's mind. As for herself, she'd added a lavender-scented oil to her bath and hoped she reminded Adam of his beloved Scottish home. If not that, then at least a pleasant Scottish flower.

Not that she was Scottish, but he was and obviously missed his home.

"Not a pleasant day at all," Emily Dowd said, mimicking her mother's disdainful air.

Remi shrugged off their dismissive glances, understanding why the Dowds were not happy to see her. She was competition for Emily, who no doubt sought Adam's affections. Well, Remi refused to be glum about it. Emily was pretty, but she wasn't particularly nice or clever, which made her completely unsuitable to be a vicar's wife, especially this vicar.

As for Lady Monkton, she was a fairly attractive woman married to a lunkhead of a husband. He wasn't cruel or prone to excessive drinking or gambling. He was just dull as dishwater. Remi was innocent, but not so innocent as to be ignorant of Lady

Monkton's intentions toward Adam. Not that he needed Remi to protect him from the unwanted advances of a hungry female.

But she did not like to think he might be receptive to the odious woman.

No, Adam was honorable. He would never take up with a married lady.

Remi was struggling for something polite to say in order to break the uncomfortable silence when Adam's housekeeper rolled in the tea cart. "Lady Remington," Adam said, turning to her, "may I impose upon you to act as my hostess?"

It was a proper request since she, despite being presently homeless, was the highest-ranking lady among them. "I would be delighted."

Also, despite her rebellious nature, her years of finishing school had served their purpose. She knew how to behave like a lady, and was glad to have given thought to her attire. She wore a gown of ivory muslin with a forest-green pelisse that highlighted her auburn hair. She looked elegant but approachable. Her hair was done up in a braided chignon at the nape of her neck, once again elegant but not too ornate. She hoped to look charming and suitably understated, not the imperious earl's daughter.

Two men hurried in as she was pouring tea for the ladies. The first gentleman was a local magistrate, Squire Claymore, a pleasant, rotund fellow who enjoyed hearing himself speak. The second was a successful local merchant by the name of Mr. Squibb who thought quite highly of himself.

Adam greeted them and motioned for them to be seated. "Shall we begin? Anyone have suggestions for our midsummer's eve festivities?"

Mr. Squibb frowned. "I wouldn't call our plans festive. We ought to be giving thanks to our Creator for providing us with our bounty. The children especially must be discouraged from behaving like heathens."

The others took turns making comments and offering sugges-tions, none of which remotely appealed to Remi. Finally, it was her turn. She cleared her throat. "I think we must hold a fair. Surely a marionette show and some games for the children would not cause any harm. I think a three-legged race would be fun. Children need to run around, especially if the weather is beautiful. Perhaps we can make faerie wings for them and crown one of them the faerie queen or king. Food and dancing for the adults."

Her suggestions were immediately voted down. "You seem to be under the misapprehension we are planning a party," Lady Monkton said with a sniff.

"Why can it not be a party? Isn't the point of this celebration to make goodness enjoyable?" Adam asked.

Remi glanced at him, hoping she hadn't embarrassed him too badly. But he did not seem in the least disgruntled, so she pressed her suggestion. "What is wrong with holding a fair at the vicarage? Food, dancing, and games, but all for charity. I mentioned faerie wings, but we can call them angel wings instead. The three-legged races can be run for charity, each participating pair designating their favorite cause. A pie-eating contest, too. I'm sure the local landowners would all be happy to donate to a church roof or new psalm books or food for a struggling family, whatever the cause designated by the winner of each event. All for a good purpose, and the children would be quite happy to participate."

"I like the idea," Adam said before anyone else could respond. "Lady Remington, you seem to have given this serious thought. Midsummer's Eve is a perfect time to bring our Wellesford families together to celebrate love of their neighbors and village. I have no doubt the Earl of Welles and Duke of Hartford would be happy to donate a few shillings to a good cause. Perhaps others would as well." He stared pointedly at the magistrate and Mr. Squibb, both of whom felt a sudden need to stare at their toes.

"The children will feel quite proud of themselves. I'm sure they will enjoy racing across the field for a good cause," Remi said.

Adam grinned at her. "Or stuff their little faces with pie to help fix our roof."

Mrs. Dowd shot to her feet. "It seems the two of you have it all worked out. Come, Emily. We are obviously not wanted here."

Adam sighed. "Do sit down, Mrs. Dowd. The fair is an excellent idea and we should all be in the planning of it together. Piety does not mean deprivation, and I certainly do not want any families in this parish to feel that attending my Sunday sermon is a chore. I particularly like the idea of involving the children in raising donations. I don't know how better to make them feel as part of the Church." He turned to Remi. "Will you take the lead in organizing the fair?"

Her eyes rounded in surprise. "Yes, I would love to."

Lady Monkton rose and walked to Adam's side, stroking his arm. "Our dear Lady Remington will not be here by the end of the week. We all know her situation. Her father will either disown her or cart her off to some impoverished nobleman to marry."

"Indeed," Emily said, coming to his side as well. "Vicar, I'll work closely with you on this matter. How can you think to ask Lady Remington? You'll be left with shambles when she suddenly disappears."

Mrs. Dowd also crowded around him. "My Emily is more than capable. We don't need Lady Remington."

Adam's committee members were quick to vote her out. Remi was heartbroken but refused to allow her disappointment to show. Adam had stood up for her. It was enough. Since everyone was already on their feet, huddling around him, she rose as well. "Thank you for inviting me, Vicar. I shall be going now."

She heard him call out to her. "Lady Remi, please."

"I must go." She refused to look back, afraid he would realize how upset she was. Nor did she wish the others to see her devastation.

But where was she to go?

She was too overset to return to Sherbourne Manor just yet. The day was nice enough. She decided to sit by the river, but this time keeping her shoes and stockings on, and not wading in.

Why had she thought anything would be different? Her father had poisoned everyone in Wellesford against her. They considered her a laughingstock and always would.

She plunked herself down on the bench and stared at the swiftly moving river current, wishing it would simply wash her away. She was not yet composed when Adam came upon her. "Thought I'd find you here," he muttered.

She kept her gaze on the water. "I'm sorry if I spoiled your meeting."

The bench groaned as he set his large frame beside her. "You were the only bright spot in that meeting. Your ideas were perfect. The children would have loved everything you suggested."

"But..."

He shrugged. "They don't know what will happen to you after the Sherbourne party, and it worries them."

"And you?" Her hands began to shake. "You must realize that what happens to me is completely in your control. I've made my feelings known to you. Indeed, I've bared my heart to you. Need I humiliate myself more?"

"Remi, you are worked up right now."

"If you accuse me of being hysterical, I will hit you. Do you not like me? Because that kiss we shared gave quite the opposite impression. But you are so caught up piling those stones around your heart, defending your fortress so no one ever gets in, that you are willing to let me go."

She rose, preparing to walk away because it was simply too painful to be close to him. "I've read the book Poppy gave me. I believe in the magic of love. I just don't know how to make you believe in it."

"Remi, wait. Don't go."

"Give me a reason to stay."

He placed a gentle hand on her arm. "You want to know more about me, don't you? Sit down and I'll tell you."

CHAPTER TEN

R EMI SHOOK HER head.

Dear heaven, had she heard right?

Was Adam really going to tell her about himself? She offered no resistance when he took her hand and led her back to the bench beside the river, keeping hold of her hand even after they sat. "I told you I had four older brothers," he said, his eyes taking on a distant look. "Two of them died in the war. One early in the Peninsular War and the other about a year before Waterloo."

She held her breath.

"We were five brothers in all. One the heir, the other the spare. The third for the military. He was the one who died early on in Spain. The fourth was meant for the Church. Then there was me, meant for nothing. So, I went against my father's wishes and joined the military, never realizing that brother number four felt the need to protect me. Instead of becoming a priest, he joined the Scots Greys shortly after I did. Callum wasn't a soldier. He was a gentle soul. That last battle…we were ambushed by the French. By the time I could fight my way to him, he'd taken a mortal blow." He buried his head in his hands, propping his bent elbows on his thighs. "I couldn't protect him. He died in my arms."

"Oh, Adam." Remi's breaths turned ragged. She fought to keep tears from streaming down her face, but his revelation had left her shattered. "I'm so sorry. You must have loved him very much."

He nodded. "I'd gone against my father's wishes, and my brother died because of it. How could I return to Inverness? Me alive and Callum gone. I did not know how else to honor him, so I joined the Church as he was always meant to do."

"Why the Church of England?"

He shrugged. "Why not? I wasn't ever returning to Scotland. I was going to bury my past and make a new life for myself. I wound up here in the Cotswolds, in this village of Wellesford. I preached forgiveness and faith but felt none of it for the longest time."

"What changed you?"

"One Christmas a few years ago. I received a sign from above." He cast her a wry smile. "I saw a vision of the Nativity. All of it, even the three Magi."

"Truly? Then you must believe in miracles."

"Perhaps, but it wasn't quite like that. No golden angels came down from on high. It had to do with Miss Billings and Dr. Carmichael. She'd fallen and hurt herself shortly before Christmas, so she could not attend the Sherbourne holiday party. She thought she would be spending the day alone, but Poppy, Olivia, and Penelope brought gifts and food to her instead. Young Pip came along, too."

He sighed and shook his head. "I had finished my duties and called upon her thinking she might need to see a friendly face. The doctor was by her bedside, and I could see he was besotted with her. I'd known he was in love with her for quite some time, but he would not say a word to her. That night, he finally did. We were all there. Miss Billings, her doctor by her side as she sat up in bed. Young Pip, who adored her, was at her other side. Olivia, Poppy, and Penelope stood at the foot of her bed. They were the three Magi bearing gifts."

"Adam," she said in a shaken whisper. "That sounds exactly like a miracle."

He cast her a wry smile. "I would not take it that far, but it was certainly a sign that a greater force does exist. It finally made me believe, made me start thinking there was a reason I was led here."

Remi's heartbeat roared in her ears. "Do you think it was for me?"

Adam ignored the question.

"How are you feeling?" he asked instead. "Are you well enough to walk back to the manor?"

She nodded.

"Good, I feel like I've been slammed in the gut by a battering ram. Don't ask me any more questions, Remi. All right?"

"Yes." She now understood him better and ached for him.

She had no brothers or sisters of her own, but knew how devastating it would be to watch helplessly as the brother you loved passed away in your arms. Having lost two out of his four beloved brothers in the turmoil of war, Adam was now linking the feeling of love to the feeling of unbearable loss.

How could she get him to surmount this?

Her dreams were of this man, this proud vicar. She hoped this talk might be some sort of breakthrough. Perhaps a revelation for him. She held onto that kernel of hope. Adam had chosen to confide in her, to trust her with his overwhelming heartbreak.

It had to mean something.

But he was wrong in believing his family did not miss him and would not want him back. His father had to be devastated. Two sons dead, and a third too ashamed to face him. If she were the father, she would have every Bow Street runner in England tracking him down through every shire and village.

No matter what happened at her party, she would make an effort to convince Adam he needed to return home to Inverness and reconcile with his family.

He did not go inside the manor house with her but took her hand for a moment at the door. "Kit is lucky to have you protecting her."

Her fox?

Why bring up that frightened little animal now?

Adam seemed to read her thoughts. "Foxes aren't the only wounded creatures you seem capable of saving."

He kissed her lightly on the cheek and strode away.

She heard nothing from him after that day.

By the night of her party, she was afraid he had changed his mind and would not attend. She was not about to let this happen, nor was she too proud to traipse across the meadow and drag him to her party. She did not care if her fine slippers were ruined or the hem of her gown was splattered with mud. It was a lovely tea rose silk that brought out her roses and cream complexion.

But it was just a possession and replaceable.

He was not.

"You look like a princess," Poppy whispered as they stood in the entry hall with Nathaniel while greeting their guests. Lavinia was next to her, holding Periwinkle in her arms, while Pip stood beside Nathaniel. "Don't worry, Remi. He'll be here," Lavinia whispered.

She hoped so.

She wanted to believe in dreams coming true.

But she gave up hope as the last of their guests arrived. The orchestra struck up a lively reel. Mr. Squibb's son claimed her for the dance. He was as full of himself as his wealthy merchant father was. His hand kept drifting lower on her waist every time they swung around. How long before he accidentally planted his sweaty palm on her backside?

But she had to keep her spirits up, remain hopeful.

Dreams do come true.

Dreams do come true.

Dreams do—

She inhaled lightly when Adam appeared in the doorway.

Oh, my heavens.

He looked splendid.

She craned her neck to follow him as he moved through the crowd toward her. He was not smiling by the time he reached the dance floor. Had he seen Mr. Squibb's odious son and the direction of his hand?

He must have, for his gaze turned surprisingly predatory.

Suddenly it was as though everything she'd read in *The Book of Love* was coming true. Adam's gaze turned dark and threatening. He began to prowl along the edges of the dance floor like a lion penned in its cage.

Was she mistaken or did his chest suddenly swell? Although she had no desire to have young Squibb's clammy hand on her backside, it was almost worth it to see how Adam would respond. But Squibb had also taken notice of Adam. His hand no longer roamed downward. Indeed, he was almost afraid to touch her.

She cast Adam a beaming smile as they twirled past him. Unfortunately, she wasn't very tall and quickly lost sight of her proud lion as she was drawn into the center of a circle of dancers.

Adam strode toward her as soon as the dance ended. Squibb the Younger had returned her to Lavinia's side and quickly left. Her heart began to pound wildly, for Adam was coming toward her and his expression was not in the least bit tame. "It's to be a waltz," Lavinia whispered excitedly.

She tried to appear calm as Adam reached her side. "I believe this dance is mine, Lady Remington."

"Yes, Vicar. I have you clearly written in my dance card." She took his offered hand, never mind that she had no dance card or even a pencil with which to write his name down.

He placed his arm around her waist and took her hand in his. "Are ye ready, R-r-remi?" he asked in his delicious brogue, his voice a deep, seductive rumble.

"I've been ready for you all of my life." This was no time to mince words. She loved him, and the only question remaining was whether he loved her.

The music started.

She closed her eyes and allowed herself to be guided by Adam's steps and the gentle touch of his hand. He was a surprisingly good dancer, quite graceful on his feet. Was it so different from the twists and turns when fighting on a field of battle? Since he was cavalry, she imagined him upon his deep-chested gray, guiding the steed left or right, forward or back with the slightest motion of his thighs, rider and horse moving as one.

"Remi, you look lost in a dream. Will you keep your eyes closed the entire dance?"

She nodded. "I'm afraid to open them. Is this real? Am I truly in your arms?"

"Aye, lass."

"You're talking like a braw Scot again. I like that. Thank you for dancing with me." She opened her eyes and smiled at him. "Will you claim me for a second?"

"And set tongues wagging?" He grinned. "Of course."

She inhaled lightly. "Adam, do you think…that is…will you–"

A commotion in the entry hall startled everyone. Someone was shouting and pushing his way through the crowd. The music trickled to a stop as the orchestra stopped playing. "Oh, no." She recognized her father's apoplectic bellow.

Adam drew her behind him as her father stormed toward them. "Remi, stay back."

"Have you not shamed me enough, you ungrateful child?" Her father tried to grab her, but Adam would not allow it, keeping himself positioned between them.

"Are you drunk, Lord Hartfield? Keep away from Remi. I won't let you harm her."

"She's my daughter. *Mine*. You have no right to come between us."

Adam wouldn't budge. "You are angry. You'll hurt her, and I cannot allow that. Come into Lord Welles' study and we'll discuss your daughter's–"

"We'll discuss nothing." He tried to push his way past Adam again, but he was a big, stubborn, immovable Scot.

"I am not turning your daughter over to you. Join me and Lord Welles in his study and we'll talk about her situation."

"Who are you to order me about? You are nothing, a nobody.

Do you think I'd ever allow a lowly vicar anywhere near my daughter?" He threw his head back and laughed. "I've had enough of her nonsense. She's coming home with me. She'll marry the man I choose. If I catch you near her again, I'll have you shot."

Remi gasped and stormed around Adam, ignoring him as he grabbed her around the waist and attempted to haul her behind him. She wriggled out of his grasp and confronted her father. "I'll shoot you first if you dare harm him! I love that man! And I–"

Oh, heavens.

She'd shouted it so everyone could hear.

If Adam did not love her, then her humiliation would be complete. Too late to take it back. It wasn't as if she could hide her feelings anyway.

Adam knew how she felt before she'd ever told him. Now everyone knew it.

Poppy, Nathaniel, Lavinia, Pip, Periwinkle, their entire Sherbourne staff, and all their invited guests were gaping at her. An oppressive silence descended upon the ballroom. Remi tipped her chin into the air. "I love him," she repeated because if she was going to take a fall, it was going to be a spectacular, humiliating plunge.

She turned to Adam and looked up to meet his gaze.

He groaned. "Remi, what are ye doing?"

"Vicar Carstairs…" She cleared her throat. "Vicar Carstairs…would you do me the honor… Um, would you give me the greatest pleasure…" She was trying to propose marriage and failing miserably. She now understood how a frightened suitor felt when laying open his heart and soul. "Because I think if we…Gretna Green…you know. They do it quick there."

She glanced at Periwinkle, wishing the dog would bark. Or pee on someone. Anything to take all eyes off her.

She closed her eyes, fighting to stave off tears.

Adam caressed her cheek. "Yes."

"What?" She opened her eyes to stare at him.

"Masterfully done, lass," he said in a whisper, but his smile was exquisitely tender. "Yes, Lady Remington. I will marry you."

A collective gasp carried through the room.

"Yes?" Had he just accepted her? Women would be wailing in the streets of Wellesford tonight. "Is that what you said? Yes?"

Her father tried to grab her, but Adam was having none of that. He stepped between them again. "No more, Lord Hartfield. Come into the study, and we'll work out the terms."

Her father burst out laughing. "Terms?" he said with bitter derision. "There will be no terms. You'll have not a shilling from me. You want my daughter? Then take her with nothing, for that's all I'll give her. Nothing. Not my wealth. Not my connections. No allowance. She'll come to you with the clothes on her back and nothing more. What do you say to that, Vicar?" He turned and whirled to face everyone. "Same goes for any of you other fortune hunters. Not so much as a crumb will you have from me."

Remi was shaking, she couldn't help it. She was angry. She was so very hurt. All her years of wanting to love this man and this is how he felt? Not even a pang of regret when tossing her into the dust bin? "Adam, I'm so sorry. I'll understand if you walk away from me."

He took her hand in his and kept a tight hold. "Not letting go of you, Remi. Not ever."

His words further infuriated her father. "Better think twice, Vicar. She's letting you go. Take her up on it because I will crush you. I'll destroy your family and all you hold dear. I'll–"

"You'll do nothing of the sort," Poppy's husband said with a growl, obviously having had enough of this scandalous display of temper in his home.

"Who's to stop me? You?" Her father raised a fist and drew it back, but Adam caught the swing before it could strike Nathaniel.

"Enough," Adam said calmly. "You'll crush no one. You'll go home and sleep off your drunken rage. Perhaps as that dense fog of stupor dissipates, you'll come to realize what a gem you have in Remi. She loves you with all her being, would have taken any scrap of affection from you and treasured it. You've had your chance and now it is mine."

He turned to Remi. "I will love you to the day I die, lass. While there is breath in me, I will honor and cherish you and the children I hope we'll be blessed to have."

Several ladies fainted.

Remi couldn't pull her gaze from Adam, but she thought Emily Dowd and Lady Monkton were among those who had thudded to the floor. Yes, there would be weeping, wailing, and fainting throughout Wellesford tonight.

"Adam, do you mean it?" she whispered, hardly daring to breathe.

"Aye, every blessed word. I'm sorry you proposed to me first. It was my intention to offer for you tonight." He kissed her lightly on the lips, the pressure of his mouth warm and delightful on hers. "As for my family, there's something I ought to have told you about them."

Her father laughed harshly. "Here it comes, Remi. Now you'll see what you've stepped into. You could have had a viscount or a baron. Perhaps an earl. But you've chosen the penniless son of a lowly Scottish crofter. Let's see how warm your threadbare clothing keeps you in the years to come."

She ignored her father and maintained her gaze on Adam. She knew he would pounce on the man if he dared harm her. *The man.* She could not think of him as her father. What parent would ever treat his child this way? "If you love your family," she said, smiling up at Adam, "then I shall love them, too."

"As I'm sure they'll love you." He was grinning at her now. "I should have told you about them sooner."

She nodded. "It isn't important. I love you for the man you are."

"A nobody," her father muttered.

Adam's smile faded as he stared at her. "Perhaps I am that, but my family is quite important in Scotland."

More snorts of disdain from her father. "Whiskey runners?"

"Aye, there's a little of that. Remi, lass, I wanted to tell you sooner." He glanced over her head to Nathaniel. "Lord Welles has always known the truth, but I asked him to keep it quiet. There's no need any longer." He sounded pained as he said, "My father…happens to be the Duke of Inverness."

More female bodies dropped. Remi was too busy making sense of what he was telling her. "Not that I'll ever inherit the title. As I said, I have older brothers and they have sons of their own. My brother Gavin is the heir and Gareth is the spare. At best I was only ever third in line. Now I believe I'm about seventh."

"You're the son of a duke?" her father said.

"Fifth son by birth order."

Remi cast him a glowing smile. "I love fifth sons."

"And I happen to love auburn-haired hoydens who save foxes. Will ye come home with me, Remi?"

"To Scotland?"

He nodded. "Aye, lass. My father will be pleased to meet my new wife. It will be good to see him and my brothers again. As you said, it's long past time we reconciled."

"It would be my pleasure."

EPILOGUE

Inverness, Scotland
July 1818

R EMI'S HEART BEAT faster as the massive castle where Adam had been raised came into view. The stone fortress overlooking the wild sea and the ruggedly beautiful highlands around it seemed to suit his temperament and she saw how his character had been formed by his upbringing here. Wild and a bit isolated. Strong and stoic.

"What do ye think, Remi?" His light brogue had returned, not out of irritation but of happiness, for his eyes were alight and he had a smile on his face as their carriage rolled into the castle courtyard and drew up beside the front entry.

"It is magnificent. I cannot wait to meet your father and brothers."

"I don't think you'll meet Gareth and his brood yet, but Gavin and his son are sure to be here."

"Little Rafe," she said with a nod. "I hope they'll like me."

He took her hand and entwined it in his. "They will, lass. I love you, Remi. Never doubt that my family will love you as well." He turned her to face him, taking a moment before the footmen came forward to open the door. "Ye're my wife, and I meant every word of my wedding vows. I will love ye forever."

He kissed her softly on the mouth, then laughed when he drew away and saw tears form in her eyes. "My family will think ye regret our marriage if they see ye crying."

She shook her head. "They will understand it is because I am so happy. Adam, in all my life I never had this sort of acceptance. And now I am to meet your family. I know they will be as wonderful as you."

She had barely spoken the words before two men and a boy came tearing out of the castle. The eldest threw open the door, hardly giving her a chance to descend before wrapping her in his big arms. "Welcome home, daughter!"

Adam laughed. "Now ye've done it, ye old goat. She will never stop crying now." While Remi hugged his father back, Adam knelt and scooped up his nephew. "Rafe? Ye've grown into a strapping lad."

The boy wrapped his arms around his uncle.

Adam then took a moment to toss Remi a wink.

She smiled back and stared at the two of them through her tears. The little one was a miniature of these Carstairs men, for Adam's brother, the duke's heir, had the same dark hair and blue eyes as Adam, and so did his son. This was Gavin Carstairs who went by the title of Marquess of Falkirk. He was slightly bigger and broader, but still quite handsome. As for their father, the Duke of Inverness, his hair may be grayer, but there was no mistaking the resemblance to all these men.

"Welcome to the family," Adam's brother said and glanced up at the sky that was now starting to turn a thunderous gray. "Ye made it just in time. Come inside quickly, for the rain here shows no mercy."

She took his arm when he held it out to her, and they hastened indoors. "What do ye think of this pile of stones, Remi?"

"I think it is heaven. The furnishings are impressive, of course. But it is the smiles on your faces that makes me love this place. I cannot wait to hear all about Adam growing up here as a boy."

The duke, who followed them alongside Adam and Gavin's little boy, chortled. "Ye mean he hasna told ye anything?"

"Oh, yes. But I have only his version. To hear him tell it, he was a saintly child."

The duke gave Adam a good-natured slap on the back. "I thought I taught ye never to lie."

Adam grinned at Remi. "I may have exaggerated the truth a bit."

"It's good to have ye back, son," the duke said, his own eyes now tearing up. "And Remi, ye'll have to tell us how ye broke through those thick stone walls Adam built around his heart. Not that I doubt yer ability. It is easy to see why he fell in love with ye. Well, we'll have lots of time to chat around the dinner table. But thank ye, lass. Ye have no idea the joy with which we received yer letter. Ye worked a miracle on this family."

Gavin, sober and steady, nodded. "Ye made a dream come true for us, Remi."

Adam now moved toward her and took her in his arms. "She was a dream come true for me as well. I always considered her beautiful and had a hard time resisting her."

She cast him a playfully chiding look. "Hah! You hid it very well. None of us had any idea, least of all me."

"I knew I loved ye for certain when ye ran into the confessional that day with yer fox." He turned to his father with a smug grin. "Ye see, Remi saves wounded creatures…and she surely saved me."

Rafe now looked up at her with big, sad eyes. The lad truly was an adorable miniature of his father, his dark hair a little more unruly and a tumble of curls, but his eyes were that striking blue. There was no overlooking how badly the boy missed a woman's touch. She recognized it, for when had her own mother ever bothered with her?

Of course, Rafe's mother must have loved him, but she had passed. Gavin was a widower and obviously tried hard to be all things to his son. Remi could see there was love between the two, for it was clear in the way the boy naturally went to his father and the tender way Gavin accepted him.

The duke understood her thoughts. "Remi, lass. Do ye think ye and Adam might settle here?"

Adam chose to reply to his father. "We'll visit ye as often as we can, that I promise. But Remi and I have made a life for ourselves in Wellesford. We hope ye'll come visit us, too. Ye'll always be welcome, all of ye."

"We would love to have you," Remi added sincerely.

What went unspoken was the loss of their two brothers. She knew Adam would talk about them to Gavin at some point during their visit. She hoped he would also find the strength to talk to his father, for the old man obviously did not hold him to blame for the death of either of them. The war had taken his sons along with thousands of other young men.

But Adam's nature was to guard and protect. Even though he was the youngest, he and Gavin must have been the biggest and strongest, and both had always felt responsible for their other siblings.

Once they were alone in their guest chambers, Adam drew her into his arms again and kissed her with deep longing. "I love ye, Remi."

She caressed his cheek. "I love you, too. I have never been seduced in a Scottish castle. I think I will quite enjoy it…with you, of course. You are the only man who fills my dreams."

"As you are the only woman in mine." He emitted a laughing groan. "I should not admit how often my dreams were filled with you before we were married. But now I have you as my bride and I can say for a certainty that having you in my bed and in my arms is far better than agonizing over you in a fantasy."

"Let's wash up and return downstairs. Your father referred to me as his daughter. *His daughter.* You have no idea how good that made me feel. I have never belonged to my own flesh and blood. Neither one of my parents ever bothered with me, nor did my mother send word to me about our marriage. But it is all right. I no longer care if they ignore me. I belong to you and that is everything. It feels good to be a Carstairs."

"We'll protect ye, Remi. Never worry that you will be alone again. You have us as your family now. But I see we will need to work on Gavin next."

"What do you mean?"

"His first marriage was one of duty. It was not a love match. However, he was always a good and loyal husband. Having found my happiness, I wish it for him as well."

"A good father, too. It is obvious how much he loves his son. And I doubt he needs our help in finding him a wife. He will know it when he meets her. Let's hope he will not be as dense as you in admitting his feelings."

"Dense, am I?" He moved to the door and bolted it, then returned with a wicked smile on his face. He glanced toward the bed. "What do ye say, lass?"

"I say you are a very naughty vicar." She kissed him lightly on the lips and then turned her back to him so he could more easily unlace her. "And you have a very wanton wife."

"All the encouragement I need." He swept her into his arms and carried her to bed. "My family will not expect us down for another half hour yet."

Remi threw her arms around him as a burst of thunder roiled the air. The rain suddenly came down harder than she had ever seen rain fall before.

"Scared, love?"

"Terrified," she said in a seductive whisper. "Good thing I have a big, handsome vicar to protect me."

"Och, ye wicked woman. Dinna give me that breathy encouragement, or I'll never let ye out of my bed."

She giggled. "Half an hour is all you get, Vicar. You had better get busy."

"Ever your obedient servant," he said, because finding each other was a dream come true for both of them.

A dream of love.

Also by Meara Platt

FARTHINGALE SERIES
My Fair Lily
The Duke I'm Going To Marry
Rules For Reforming A Rake
A Midsummer's Kiss
The Viscount's Rose
Earl Of Hearts
If You Wished For Me
Never Dare A Duke
Capturing The Heart Of A Cameron

BOOK OF LOVE SERIES
The Look of Love
The Touch of Love
The Taste of Love
The Song of Love
The Hope of Love (novella)
The Scent of Love
The Kiss of Love
The Chance of Love
The Gift of Love
The Heart of Love
The Promise of Love
The Wonder of Love
The Journey of Love
The Treasure of Love
The Dance of Love
The Remembrance of Love (novella)

DARK GARDENS SERIES
Garden of Shadows
Garden of Light
Garden of Dragons

Garden of Destiny
Garden of Angels

LYON'S DEN SERIES
The Lyon's Surprise
Kiss of the Lyon
Lyon in the Rough

THE BRAYDENS
A Match Made In Duty
Earl of Westcliff
Fortune's Dragon
Earl of Kinross
Pearls of Fire
Aislin
Gennalyn
A Rescued Heart
Earl of Alnwick
Tempting Taffy
All I Want For Christmas (novella)

DeWOLFE PACK ANGELS SERIES
Nobody's Angel
Kiss An Angel
Bhrodi's Angel

About the Author

Meara Platt is a USA TODAY bestselling author and an Amazon UK All-Star. Her favorite place in all the world is England's Lake District, which may not come as a surprise since many of her stories are set in that idyllic landscape, including her award-winning paranormal romance Dark Gardens series. Learn more about the Dark Gardens and Meara's lighthearted and humorous Regency romances in her Farthingale series and Book of Love series, or her warmhearted Regency romances in her Braydens series by visiting her website at www.mearaplatt.com.